THE
GRAYSPACE
BEAST

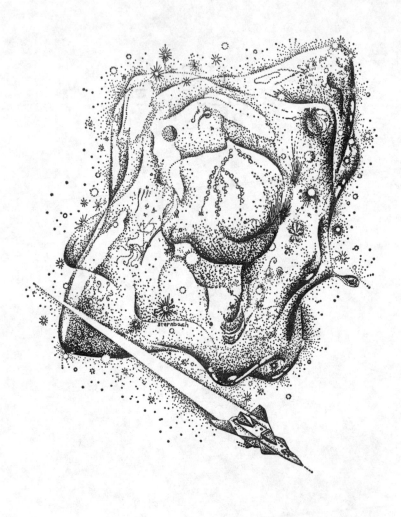

THE
GRAYSPACE
BEAST

GORDON EKLUND

Illustration by Rick Sternbach

DOUBLEDAY & COMPANY, INC.

GARDEN CITY, NEW YORK   1976

Library of Congress Cataloging in Publication Data

Eklund, Gordon.
The Grayspace beast.

I. Title.
PZ4.E3477Gr   [PS3555.K5]   813'.5'4
ISBN 0-385-11547-4
Library of Congress Catalog Card Number 75-36591

THE
GRAYSPACE
BEAST

ONE

"Which reminds me of a story," I said, facing the children.

"What story this time, old man?" asked one.

"Well, have any of you heard of the grayspace beast?" I asked.

"Hell, yes," said one of the older ones—a boy, most likely. "Have you ever heard of your own mother?"

I couldn't help smiling. "Well, it's been a time, I do admit."

"Which has? Your mother or the story?"

"Well, both," I admitted. "The story's an awfully long one, too."

"And violent?"

"At times."

"Sorrowful?"

"Considerably."

"Sexy?"

"Never."

"True?"

"Most assuredly."

"Oh, bull," cried a chorus.

"No, it is true," I protested. "You see, I was there and can remember every last detail as vividly as yesterday," I added, despite the fact that the school curriculum insisted that this knowledge be kept secret till much later. Unfortunately, I had a reputation to overcome.

"Then shut up and tell it."

I grinned to myself. "All of it?"

"No, just the middle third," said a sarcastic girl.

"I had this story from one who had no right to tell it," I went on, obliviously.

"Yeah, yourself, old man."

"Let me begin by setting the scene."

While the fake pink sawdust of Paradise Planet's gay midway swirled delicately about his slender ankles, Commander Kail Kaypack of the Grayspace Stellar Service stood hunched over and watched through hooded eyes as the new fleecies from a hundred worlds materialized one by one upon the flat, bare scancircle in front of him. As each newcomer tumbled into view, Kaypack studied the person's clothes and features with a calculating, skillful eye. Here came a dark woman two and a half meters high, as slim and high-boned as a cult priestess and wearing a toe-length gown that caught the dim midway light and erupted in a golden sunburst of glittering light. A damn rich woman, calculated Kaypack, and bored. The hard, cold tilt of her black eyes loudly proclaimed that few thrills were alien to her. After a quick glance, Kaypack turned away and ignored this woman; she lay far beyond the boundaries of his present needs.

But now, in rapid, dizzying succession, materialized a whole huge family. The father wore rags and lacked half of his right arm, while the children (there were nine) huddled close to the bare feet of their cowering mother. Backworlders, recognized Kaypack, the sort of virgin settlers for whom the term "fleecie" had been coined. Painfully, Kaypack faced away. He would not touch them. *I cheat and steal, I do not exploit;* that was his current motto. Other sharpies would surely grab and fleece them. Kaypack retained a measure of his innocence.

Ah. His body stiffened as a young couple materialized within the circle. From the size and splendor of the jewels they wore, Kaypack guessed that together they must own a planet. Instinctively he hastened forward to intercept them.

"Greetings," said Kaypack, inserting his body directly in the woman's path. "May I welcome you to Paradise Planet?"

"You may get the hell out of our way," said the man. Except for the many jewels, he was nude. His body shone with the lean virility of a young ox.

"Don't be rude," the woman corrected.

"With this thief?"

"With this man."

Kaypack bowed quickly, removing his plumed silvercap with a sleek flourish. "Commander Kail Kaypack of the Grayspace Stellar Service. I have a gift for you."

"We don't want any of your damn gifts." The man started to move past.

The woman stood her ground and smiled at Kaypack, who immediately reversed his original estimate: This woman owns a planet, he decided.

"What gift?" she asked.

"Merely this." Kaypack hastily removed one of the tickets from an inner pocket of his silversuit and presented it to the woman. "A concession as thrilling as any midway attraction," he explained. "With my compliments."

The woman studied the ticket while her husband shuffled his feet and glowered. "What is a grayspace ride?" she asked.

"The concession to which I referred." Kaypack knew it was dangerous to remain here talking too long. "The fourth quadrant, the ninth lot."

Fortunately, the man chose this moment to voice his suppressed rage. He reached out to grab the woman and managed to obtain a grip on her shaking wrist. "Damn it, Tonio, we came here to gamble, not to go on stupid rides." He tried to drag her toward the midway. "Are you coming or aren't you?"

"Let go of me and I'll consider it," she said, resisting coldly.

Burning with anger, the man let her go.

She turned toward Kaypack and bowed. "Thank you very much for the ticket."

Kaypack bowed in return. "You are very welcome."

She held out her hand to the man. "Now we will gamble."

Once the two were gone, Kaypack turned swiftly for the safety of the shadows, but he had barely managed to move both feet when a firm hand fell on his shoulder.

"I've got you, Kaypack," said a voice.

"Oh, hello, Rickard." Kaypack turned to face the man who had spoken. (Rickard Welch, chief security agent for the Paradise Planet Syndicate.)

"Give me those goddamn tickets," said Welch, thrusting out one well-padded hand.

"Tickets?" said Kaypack, pretending confusion. "What tickets?"

"The ones you just passed to those two fleecies." The outstretched flesh quivered.

Never lie when you won't be believed: this was another of Kaypack's mottos. He produced the tickets. "A harmless prank, Rickard."

"And pure thievery." Welch studied the tickets with a savage eye. "You'll be suspended for this."

(The concessions along Paradise Planet's midway did not charge admission. They existed only to draw customers to the syndicate's lucrative casinos. Each concessionaire, including Kaypack, received a daily stipend based on the number of customers drawn.)

"But, Rickard, can't you—?"

"This isn't your first offense, Kaypack. I'm sorry." Clutching the tickets tightly in his puffed hand, Welch moved into the crowd.

Desperate, Kaypack pursued. "But, Rickard, think of the children."

Puzzled, Welch stopped. "Children? What children?"

"The ones who come here to see me." Kaypack waved at the tattered fabric of his wrinkled silversuit. "I'm a hero to them. How can you disappoint so many innocents?"

"Kaypack," said Welch, bluntly, "the only children who

ever heard of you died of old age fifty years before I was born."

"No!" cried Kaypack in anguish.

"Yes," said Welch. And twisting gracelessly upon a plump ankle, he went away alone.

When he reached the fourth quadrant, the ninth lot, Kail Kaypack approached his alien helper, Veador, who stood among the loose pink sawdust that fronted the concession. Directly behind Veador was a bright green plastic wall with a round opening gaping in the center of it. Above the hole, imprinted upon the wall itself, a neon sign flashed in glittering silver:

> GRAYSPACE CRUISE!
> *Experience the Wonder of Yestertimes:*
> *Be a Stellar!*

"Well," Kaypack asked Veador, "any business?"

"Not in recent moments, my commander." Veador might have passed for a human being, except that his skin was green, his hair a lilac shade, and his tail nearly a meter in length. One hundred eighty years before, Veador had served as Kaypack's crew chief aboard an interplanetary transport ship. Since then, the two had never been apart. Kaypack sometimes thought, in a forgotten moment, that he might have purchased Veador as a slave.

"Not a young man and woman who bicker constantly? Dressed nearly naked?"

"No one matching that description, my commander."

"Damn!"

At times the communication between Kaypack and Veador seemed nearly telepathic in its intensity. "You were apprehended passing the tickets?"

Kaypack lowered his chin in shame. "Welch caught me personally."

"That is terrible, my commander."

"He intends to have me suspended."

"And our debt?"

Kaypack let his chin touch his chest. "It will fall due."

"We cannot pay it."

"Then we'll have to work it off."

"It is a very large amount, my commander. To be exact—"

"Don't be." Veador possessed a very mathematical mind. "I don't intend to stick here to find out."

"But we cannot go, my commander."

"And we can't stay."

"We lack the scanfee."

"Then we'll have to . . ." Kaypack hated to have his impotence show. "We'll have to find another way."

As soon as he reached the secluded sanctuary of his private womb, Kail Kaypack threw himself down onto the soft, squishy floor and, as always, considered the question of an autobiography.

If he ever actually came to compose such a book (a highly unlikely event), he intended to divide the narrative into three unequal sections. The first, which he expected to entitle "My Apprenticeship in Living," would deal with his birth and life upon old Earth, his long-dead parents and siblings, and finally his first space voyage, at the age of fourteen years, to Earth's ancient moon. It was during the course of this trip, seeing the Earth round and blue and whole for the first time, that he had decided definitely to spend the remainder of his life in space as a member of the Grayspace Stellar Service. The sight of that antique blue sphere had proved to him that an infinite number of similar worlds existed elsewhere in the universe and that life would never be worth enduring unless the experience of this vision could be repeated again and again as the ugly years rolled past.

The second and longest section of the autobiography, "The Stellar," would describe the two centuries in which Kaypack had commanded a variety of grayspace cruisers. In those two hundred years he had visited and explored nearly a thousand virgin planets. He would write of many of these and further attempt to describe the gray dimension itself, that empty second universe beyond normal space and time where a man could zip through a thousand parsecs in less time than it took a cat to wink an eye. This section would eventually conclude with his arrival upon the mysterious and inhabited planet Radius. Although he had spent three hundred years there, and left only to find that his life (and the stellar service) had ended in the interim, he was bound by a sworn oath not to reveal any of the events of his stay there.

So that was part of the reason why he would never actually write the book of his life. The rest was contained in the third and concluding section of the story, "My Apprenticeship in Dying." Who (least of all Kaypack) would wish to recall a single one of these last horrible years? And they weren't done yet. He was living them this very instant.

When Veador arrived in the womb, he gazed at Kaypack stretched upon the floor and frowned deeply. "I have been forced to darken our concession," he announced, dropping heavily to the floor and tucking his tail between his thighs.

Kaypack pretended to be unconcerned. "Welch, I suppose," he said, not looking up.

"He brought a syndicate directive."

Kaypack laughed suddenly. "He'll learn." He rolled onto his back and stared at the ceiling. "In time, they'll all learn."

Veador looked troubled. "Sir?"

Kaypack glared at him. "The beast, you idiot. Have you forgotten?"

"The grayspace beast?"

"Aye, Veador, aye." Again Kaypack laughed, a shrill giggle of vicious delight. "As the last stellar left alive, only I know the truth of that antique tale. There is a beast, Veador —I have often seen it with my own good eyes. The beast dwells in the gray universe, that place where no living thing can exist, the cosmic wastes. Who has not heard tell of the stellar crew emerging mad to a man from the gray wastes and bearing a lunatic tale of a silver glittering creature as large as a small moon? Aye, Veador, I have seen the grayspace beast and I know that it is evil."

"Yes, my commander," Veador said softly.

"And I also know that it soon must grow weary. Our cruisers no longer prowl the emptiness of its domain. The beast is lonely, Veador. How long till it grows impatient?"

"I wouldn't know, my commander."

"Soon, Veador, soon. The beast will emerge from its lair and come here to shred and rend the people of the thousand inhabited worlds. That will be a dismal day, Veador. A dismal day for you, for me, and for Rickard Welch."

"Yes, sir."

Kaypack laughed without restraint. "So you see how we have nothing to fear, Veador. The beast is on our side and we are thus invincible."

Veador looked very sad. He hung his head and said, "Yes, my commander, that is true."

I raised my eyes and gave the lot of them a big wink. "There's your grayspace beast for you."

One of the older boys groaned. "We weren't talking about the crazy ravings of an old coot."

"I'll have something better for you later."

"Like what?"

"How about the beast in person?"

I saw I had eroded their faith in me. "We'll wait," said one.

"I'm afraid you'll have to," I put in quickly, "because right now I'm leaving Kaypack and his beast behind for a moment and going to another world."

"Another story?"

"Same story, different planet, different character."

"What kind of story is this, anyway?"

"I told you: a long one."

"A stupid one, so far."

"Well, listen," I said, "and maybe it'll grow on you."

"Yeah, like a fungus."

"Or a disease," said a girl.

When they were silent, I went on.

While his mother lay dying in the village behind, Darcey crouched at the edge of the forest pool and peered across the pale surface at the rippling circles where the big fish were jumping. He regretted that he had neglected to bring his hook and pole with him, and yet somehow fishing seemed not wholly appropriate for the day. Even the fish themselves appeared to sense this; Darcey had never seen them so bold and defiant.

Sung emerged from the woods behind and Darcey turned to see if he had brought any word. Sung was not a human being. He stood three full meters off the ground, and his skin, unlike that of Darcey and his mother, was a dull, bloodless shade of gray. Sung was a native of this planet. Darcey's mother called the world Radius.

"Has anything happened yet?" Darcey asked softly, quietly concealing any emotion he might feel.

Sung whirled and pointed a slender finger back toward the village.

"She wants me?"

Sung nodded.

"Then she's not dead yet?"

Sung shook his head.

"You're positive?"

Again Sung nodded, a sharp snap of his narrow chin.

Darcey stood with a sigh. He had somehow hoped it would be over by now and he would no longer have to worry about how he should feel. He knew from the many books he had read that he ought to feel sad; there was an emotion called grief that should be infecting his whole spirit like the searing rays of the summer sun. But, during the entirety of his life till now, Darcey had known only one other creature to die, and that was his father, so many years ago that Darcey could barely recall the event. Now Mother was dying, too, and Darcey did not know how he should feel.

Sung was no help. He led the way silently through the thick, noisy woods.

After they had gone a short distance, Darcey could not help uttering what lay at the top of his mind. "When Mother is dead," he asked, "won't that make me the only human being on Radius?"

Without slowing his pace, Sung nodded sharply.

"Then," said Darcey, "I'll be the same as you. I'll be alone then and not really different."

Sung shrugged ambiguously, hurrying on.

Darcey matched his pace. "What I mean is, when I'm alone, there'll be no need for me not to climb Gorgan Mount."

Sung shook his head—sharply.

"Why not? I'm nineteen seasons. Mother says so."

Sung stopped so suddenly that Darcey bumped into his rear. With a savage wave of the hand, Sung thrust out a finger, indicating the village ahead.

"All right, but . . . but . . . I don't want to be alone."

Inside the dark interior of the wooden hut they shared, Darcey found his mother bundled in soft taga leaves. A sharp odor, like urine, stung his nostrils. Breathing shallowly, Darcey kissed his mother's cold lips.

"I'm dying," she murmured, a descending whisper.

"Sung told me."

"Things . . ." She took a breath. "Things I must tell you."

He turned his face so that his ear pressed close to her lips. In a flash he had seen her face, once round and pink, slashed by the stiff wires of standing veins. He remembered their years together. "Tell me."

"When I die . . ." she began.

"Today," he said.

"When I die today, you must leave this planet."

"No!" He sprang away from her.

"Darcey, don't."

"But I can't leave."

"There's a way. Sung will show you afterward. This isn't our world, Darcey. The elders let us stay, your father and I, because they were afraid we would tell—show other humans where this planet was."

"Then, if they make me go," Darcey said defiantly, "I'll tell, too."

"No, you won't."

"I will!"

"You don't know where Radius is. You couldn't tell anyone anything."

"I could!" But he knew that wasn't true.

Her breath came quicker now as she struggled to speak loudly enough for him to hear. "You'll be sent to another planet, one where humans live. When you get there, find Commander Kaypack. Do you remember him?"

"He came to Radius with you but left."

"Find him. Talk to him. And when you do, tell him this: 768G 45098 TK. That is a co-ordinate. Sung told it to me. Say it."

He replied sullenly, "768G 45098 TK. What is a co-ordinate?"

"It's a new way of getting from one spot in the galaxy to another. Without using a ship."

He laughed complacently. "That's silly."

"Sung will tell you the rest."

"An elder can't talk."

"Listen to him. And—and my pillow. When I'm gone, reach underneath and you'll find some colored paper. It's money, Darcey. Be sure to take it with you and give it to Kaypack."

"I know about money, from books," Darcey said proudly.

"Good. And now—please—stay with me. Stay until it's over, Darcey."

He remained angry with her for what she had said, but still, it was too late to go walking in the woods. "All right, Mother."

"And talk to me."

"What about?"

"Anything you like."

"I could tell you about when I went fishing yesterday at dawn."

"I'd like to hear that."

So Darcey told her. Later, he also told her about the pool in the forest, the boldly jumping fish, and the way Sung had come out of the woods. As he spoke, her eyes drifted shut and he decided she was no longer listening, but when he stopped talking, she instantly opened her eyes and pleaded silently with him to go on.

As he continued to talk, Darcey thought he might actually be experiencing grief. There was a pain somewhere in his chest, and his throat hurt, too, though that might only be from the talking. He kept looking at Mother and soon was staring and then his eyes hurt. He shed tears. The pain grew worse and spread.

Eventually he stopped talking again. This time Mother said nothing. She did not open her eyes. Darcey knew she was dead.

Much later—the night had nearly gone and dawn must be threatening outside—Sung poked his lean head through the opening of the hut and, when he saw Darcey's mother lying stiff and silent, came inside.

Darcey had lighted a fire earlier but the flames had by now been reduced to a few glowing embers.

"She's dead," Sung said, speaking for the first time since Darcey had known him. On Radius, the elders never used words. Only the children talked, and, once each of them climbed Gorgan Mount and returned alive, he stopped, too.

"Do I have to leave Radius?" Darcey asked, recalling what his mother had told him.

"You will be sent to a world called Paradise Planet."

"Why, Sung?"

"Because you are not one of us and because you have a mission to perform."

"What?"

"You are to meet with a man named Kaypack and explain to him how to recover the grayspace cruiser he left with us many years ago."

"The co-ordinate?" asked Darcey.

"Then she told you."

"About Kaypack, too."

"Then all I need tell you is the message you are to deliver to Kaypack. Tell him that the ship is to be used by him to slay the grayspace beast. Tell him you are to help him."

"The grayspace beast?" said Darcey, puzzled.

"Will you remember that message?"

"Yes, of course. But, Sung, I don't understand it."

The elder shrugged.

Darcey understood that this meant Sung was finished talking. Glancing at his mother's body, he felt for the first time how truly alone he was. Other human beings? Worlds where he would be the same and not always different? The concept dimly stirred him.

"Sung," he said suddenly, "I think I'm ready to go away."

Without word or gesture, Sung turned and went out the hut door.

With a last backward glance, Darcey followed Sung into early-morning dimness. The grayspace beast, he wondered quizzically. Darcey knew what grayspace was—his mother had told him and there were books—and he also knew the meaning of beast. How did the two words fit together?

"Very funny," said a boy.

"Why?" I asked. "It's not supposed to be."

"This guy Darcey," said another boy, "is he really as dumb as you make him out?"

"To me he's not dumb."

"Why? Are you him?"

I smiled slowly. "Do I act dumb, too?"

A girl interrupted: "I think he's Kaypack."

"There's no proof of that," I said.

"Then which is it?"

"Why should it have to be either?"

"Because, how else do you know so much about what happened? You know what they were thinking and what they said."

"Maybe somebody else told me."

"Like Darcey?"

"Sure, except maybe Darcey told somebody who told somebody else who told another person who finally told me."

"You said the story was true."

"It is."

"You can't prove it unless you were there."

"First I have to introduce another character."

"Yourself?" said the girl.

"The beast?" asked a boy.

"Not yet. That comes later. This is just a girl—a very pretty young girl."

"Isn't that trite?"

"What?"

"Making the girl pretty."

"But she was."

"I just don't think you should rub it on our faces. We can appreciate subtlety. Like with Radius. We can figure things out for ourselves."

"I'll try to remember that."

"You shouldn't underestimate your audience."

I shook my head at the whole precocious bunch. "I'm sorry."

Once again tonight, as she mechanically manipulated the shells, Nova (a very pretty young girl) felt her soul twist free from the confines of her body and rise gently upward till it came to rest against the glittering silver ceiling high above the casino floor. Neither of the two customers who faced her across the green-felt tabletop noticed the sudden disappearance of her soul. One of them, the man, simply pointed at the middle shell. "It's there," he said, winking cryptically at the sour-faced young woman beside him.

"If it is," the woman said, "it'll be the first time."

Automatically Nova pressed the red button that flipped the middle shell. "Sorry," she said, indicating the empty tabletop. Swiftly she collected the man's bet. "Care to try again?" she asked politely.

"Why? Haven't you stolen enough from me tonight?" asked the man.

"Now, now," the woman cautioned. "Don't lose your temper. We don't want to make anyone mad at us."

"Why not? I've already lost half a fortune here."

"You have, dear?" asked the woman, raising her eyebrows in surprise. "I never knew you were that rich."

"Don't be funny, Tonio," he said.

"Why shouldn't I? It was your idea to gamble, not mine. I told you we should have gone riding on that grayspace thing."

"With that old thief?"

"You prefer a younger one?" The woman pointed at Nova.

"I didn't mean it that way."

"Then how did you mean it?"

Nova waited patiently for them to subside. Tilting her head, she stared at her soul dangling above. The blistering turmoil of the casino washed over her. The place was packed wall-to-wall with fleecies tonight. Someone was growing rich. It wasn't Nova.

"Start again," said the man. "I'll bet"—he reached toward his loinstrap and withdrew a roll of creased bills—"this much." The man never bothered to look to see how much he had wagered.

Nova swiftly inserted the green pea (a small emerald, actually) under one shell, arranged all three, and depressed the button that set them spinning. Because she disliked this man more than most, she allowed the spinning to continue a few seconds longer than usual.

"It's there," said the man, pointing to the left shell.

The woman giggled into her hand.

Nova pushed the button. Again, the shell was empty.

"Damn," said the man. He got ready to bet again.

Nova saw that her soul was moving. It drifted across the flat ceiling like a submarine slicing the smoke-filled air. "I'm sorry," she said, standing abruptly. "I'm closing."

"Wait." The man gripped her wrist tightly. "Not until I've won my money back."

A friend had once shown Nova a place on the human wrist where, if you pressed it firmly with your thumb, the whole hand went numb. Nova pressed this place.

The man screamed.

As quick as a spinning shell, Nova darted underneath the table and raced toward the cluttered middle of the casino. Behind her, she heard the man shouting and the woman laughing.

She did not pause. Spotting the nearest exit chute, Nova hurried that way. Her soul came down from the ceiling and eagerly merged with her body. Nova knew this might very well mean the end of her job here—she had been warned the last time—but she also knew she couldn't stand it a moment longer. She had to get outside, had to see the sky (even if it was fake), had to breathe some clean air.

The chute, when she sprang for it, carried her gently down nine stories to the midway below. The huge bulk of the casino glowered behind. With a swift glance at the star-studded sky, Nova pushed quickly into the crowd of fleecies who thronged the midway like so many green peas hunting for shells to conceal them. She decided to walk at random. It was simple freedom she sought; the exact geographical location did not matter. She shivered with the chill, sucked in the sweet air, and studied the hollow night sky.

But—*oops*.

Suddenly in her wanderings, Nova sprang for cover. Hidden by the shadow of a hulking midway booth, she watched Rickard Welch, chief security agent for the syndicate, wobble languidly past. His tiny, dim eyes raked the dark corners around him. Nova cowered deeply. Welch was searching for someone. Her? Had he heard the news so soon?

Welch had nearly gone past when a cold hand touched her naked shoulder from behind. Nova let out a sharp, involuntary yip and spun angrily.

She saw a gangling, skinny boy of eighteen or twenty, with bony knees, huge blue eyes, and tanned brightworld skin. "Excuse me, but I wondered if—"

"You idiot," Nova whispered sharply. She glanced frantically toward the midway but Welch had already disappeared among the churning mob. "What the hell are you doing?" she demanded of the boy.

"I just wondered if you could help me," he said.

"Do I look like a helpmate?" But her anger evaporated the moment she detected the absurdity of his open, toothy grin. This boy, she suddenly understood, was the sharpie's dream come true: the ultimate fleecie in the flesh.

"I'm sorry." He started to back away.

Nova sprang for him. "No, no. It's me who should be sorry." She gripped his arm tenderly. "And I am—I really am."

He showed her his toothy smile again. "I'm Darcey." He spoke stiffly, enunciating unexpected syllables.

"Nova." She vainly attempted to match the width of his smile. "What help do you need?" She drew him nearer to her, more closely concealed by shadow.

"Well," he said, "there's this man—" He stopped and his

eyes grew even wider as the sky above flashed through a series of flickering color changes: black, blue, red, yellow, then black again. Nova knew that this meant it was now midnight by the local clock.

"What man?" she asked.

"What?" said Darcey, pointing at the sky as though a miracle had occurred.

"Oh, that happens every night. Don't let it throw you. This man . . ."

His features remained distorted by wonder. Nova snapped her fingers to draw him down to reality. Darcey blinked, shook his head, and said, "Kaypack. Commander Kail Kaypack of the Grayspace Stellar Service. Do you know him?"

"Sure." Everyone on Paradise Planet knew that old coot. "What do you want with him?"

"There's something I must give him." Darcey opened his left fist and abruptly answered Nova's prayers. In the palm of his hand, bunched into an oblong ball, sat a wad of currency the size of a grown-man's heart. "And also I must talk to him."

Nova pointed at the money. "After you give him that, he may never talk again."

"Why?" Darcey wrinkled his brow. "Is it dangerous?"

Nova realized she had already said more than was necessary. Reaching out cautiously, she closed Darcey's hand around the wad of money. "Suppose you tell me all about it, then I'll tell you the parts you may not understand."

"I don't know if I should." Darcey showed his first sign of reluctance. "I'm only supposed to tell Commander Kaypack himself."

"But I'm his best friend," said Nova.

"Still . . . Wait—I have an idea. Why don't you take me to Commander Kaypack, I can talk to him, then we can both tell you everything when I'm done?"

"I'm not sure Commander Kaypack is here right now. I

think"—she creased her brow in the effort to recall—"he may be on another planet." Nova did not want to talk to this boy—she wanted to fleece him.

"Oh, no, he's not," said Darcey, flashing his big grin once more. "I already asked a policeman and he said Commander Kaypack was home at the grayspace concession. If you'll just take me there, I'll try to find him."

"I suppose that's best," Nova said reluctantly, as her best plans evaporated in a *poof*. She had intended to invite Darcey to her womb and fleece him there. She stood up. "Come on— let's go."

"You're not angry?" he asked as they moved through the crowded midway.

"No. Why should I be?" Nova kept a wary eye peeled for Welch and his minions.

"I don't know, but you're acting like you are."

"Oh, no." Nova showed him a false smile. "I was just worried, not angry. Have you ever actually met Commander Kaypack?"

"No, but my mother and father did."

"I bet that was a long time ago."

"Yes," Darcey said, the look of wonder revisiting his face. "How did you know?"

"Kaypack." Nova hurried on, driven by sudden, brilliant inspiration. "He's changed so much—I don't quite know how to say this—he's deteriorated enormously since he came here. I don't like to call any man a cheat or thief, but with poor Kaypack it's hard to say anything else."

"You mean he steals?"

"Constantly. Jewels, money, precious goods. When I was a young girl he stole my innocence."

"How could he ever do that?"

"Listen," she said, insinuating herself close to him, like a conspirator, "and I'll tell you everything."

While Veador stood passively in front of the grayspace concession, the sky above flickered red and gold, announcing the arrival of one o'clock. A gentle wind swirled the sawdust, and the occasional passing fleecie barely glanced at the silent alien. Veador let his tail thump bleakly against the ground. He thought of his commander and the terrible lives they both now endured.

Veador loved Kail Kaypack in a manner so deep that no mere human being could ever possibly comprehend it. When one human loved another, the passion flowed from the other's character, who he was and never what, but Veador loved Kaypack because Kaypack was his commander and thus his love could never lessen, for Kaypack would always be his commander, and who he was at any given moment never mattered.

"To love someone," a human said, "he must love you in return."

"And if he does not?" asked Veador, who was keenly aware that Kaypack did not love him.

"Then you cannot love him, either."

"And if I do?"

"But you can't."

"But I do."

Humans were not stupid, but almost all were blind. They recognized the massive objects of the universe but failed to notice the shadows each cast. To Veador, the shadow of a rock was no less real than the rock itself. A human said, if you loved a shadow, then you did not truly love at all, but Veador believed the shadow was the essence of the form, and this made his love the purest and deepest form of all.

"Veador, I need your help," said a breathless voice.

Glancing up, Veador recognized Nova, a young woman who served as a sharpie in the main syndicate casino.

"The concession is closed at Welch's request," said Veador.

"I don't care about that." She lowered her voice significantly whenever anyone chanced to stray past. "In fact, that's even better."

"What is better?" Veador generally disliked all human beings because of their blindness and ignorance.

"Look, Kaypack isn't lurking around, is he?"

"My commander is resting within his womb."

"Terrific. You see, it's really your help I need. I've got this fleecie and he's packing a wad as thick as your tail is long. I want to divest him."

Veador knew enough of human nature to conceal his contempt. "Why not divest him yourself, Nova?"

She sighed dramatically. "Because this guy's really a weird piece. He wants to see the grayspace ride—that's all he'll talk about—and the damn midway's jumping tonight. So I brought him here. We'll slip him inside the ride, and then he'll get divested in there where nobody can notice."

Veador shook his head wearily. "My commander disapproves of thievery."

"I'll give you ten per cent."

Automatically, Veador said, "I cannot."

"Twenty."

Veador forced himself to think. Wasn't it true that money, or the lack of it, lay at the very root of all his present problems? If the syndicate debt could be paid, then Welch would very likely relent and allow the concession to open again. He knew that Commander Kaypack could not bear the ugly burden of forced confinement at his present age. In order to save the man he served, Veador would willingly ignore certain human moralities. "This wad of money—it is substantial?"

"Big enough to bug your eyes out," said Nova.

"Then I will do it—for an even split."

"Fifty-fifty?" She showed her astonished disgust. "Damn it, I found him and brought him here."

"The concession is mine."

"Kaypack's."

"It is either fifty-fifty or nothing," Veador said haughtily. "I cannot violate my commander's ethics for less."

Nova glanced frantically past her shoulder. Apparently she

had hidden her fleecie there—somewhere in the shadows. "All right—you win—it's fifty-fifty. Now hurry up and turn on the concession. I'll be right back with the fleecie and bring him inside. As soon as you see us, jump him and grab the wad. I'll tell him later it was a monster."

"We can only hope that Mr. Welch does not happen to wander past and notice the lights."

"I saw him earlier and I think he's busy. Come on, Veador, we've got to be quick about it."

He nodded and wandered off to activate the concession. Once he had done that, plodding around to the rear of the plastic structure, he slipped inside through a back door. Picking a careful path through the humming, beeping, whirring maze of gadgets, lights, and machinery, he reached the main control room and paused there. Seeking cover behind a wide viewscreen, he patiently awaited the arrival of Nova and her fleecie.

In spite of his total knowledge, Veador never fully succeeded in convincing himself that all of what he now saw around him was unreal. Kaypack had personally designed and built the entire concession, and every part of it—the tubes and tunnels, control room and crew quarters, star maps and viewscreens, even the nine crewmen themselves—perfectly matched a reality long since vanished. When Kaypack himself came here and sat, he often wept real tears of regret, and Veador thought he could understand why.

Hearing the approach of hasty feet, Veador peered cautiously past the edge of the viewscreen. Inside the control room, two crew members were studying a star chart and preparing to jump into grayspace. Nova halted, grabbed her fleecie's arm, and said, "Look, there it is."

"There's what?" said the boy, gazing blankly at the room.

"The control room. The grayspace cruiser. The crew. Look"—she pointed at the viewscreen opposite the one behind which Veador lurked—"there's a comet streaming past."

"Where?" The boy moved across the room until the tip of his nose nearly touched the screen. "It's blank."

"No," said Nova, her confusion showing as she hurried to his side. "Don't you smell the fresh oxygen? Can't you hear the humming engine? Can't you see the crew and everything?"

The fleecie turned. "All I see is a big, empty room. What are you trying to prove? This isn't the grayspace ride."

"But you saw the sign."

"That was outside. I don't see anything in here." The boy broke free from Nova's grasp and threw himself down in a chair already occupied by a visual replica of a crew member. Veador winced at the painful sight.

Just then, the cruiser slipped into grayspace. A wave of utter blankness swept over all four viewscreens and an aura of sudden emptiness prevaded the room. Veador shivered bleakly and Nova looked disturbed, but the boy seemed unmoved.

"Don't tell you didn't see that, either?" said Nova.

"See what?" asked the boy.

Aware that something terrible had gone wrong but unable to understand what, Veador took decisive action. Springing out from behind the concealing screen, he dashed straight for the boy, who held one fist clenched in his lap. That must be where the money's hidden, thought Veador, and he directed his charge that way.

At the very last possible moment, the boy slipped out of the chair and Veador crashed head first into it. "Hey," cried the boy, "this is pretty good! It's an alien, isn't it? I can even smell him."

Gingerly Veador picked himself up off the floor. He moved forward to stalk his prey. Wearing a big grin, the boy waved him close. The ship jumped out of grayspace. The viewscreens filled with starlight.

"Get him, Veador," whispered Nova.

Veador sprang. Once more, the boy was too quick. He

skipped aside. Plummeting past, Veador slammed his snout hard against the floor. His eyes filled with tears. He moaned in rage and anguish.

Somewhere behind him, the boy laughed in sheer delight. "This is wonderful. This is fun."

Balancing upon his tail, Veador slowly regained his feet. Hands extended, he staggered forward. This time the boy didn't budge. Nova sucked in her breath in grim anticipation. Veador edged closer . . . closer . . .

"Veador—halt!"

Veador spun and saw the figure of his commander outlined in the nearest doorway.

"Why, there's another one," said the boy, pointing an excited finger at Kaypack, who wore his silversuit and plumed cap. "That one's a stellar."

Advancing into the room, Kaypack removed his cap with a flourish. "The last of the grayspace stellars," he said, "at your service, sir."

"And he talks, too," the boy said wondrously.

"And he's real too," said Nova. "Darcey, meet Commander Kail Kaypack."

Meanwhile, the control room had been invaded by a flock of three-eyed aliens, who now engaged the human crew in a running nervegun battle. Veador shifted delicately on his feet as the deadly needles whizzed past.

"Commander Kaypack," said the boy in an awestricken voice. "I—I'm Darcey." His fist opened and he held out the wad of currency. "I was sent here to see you."

The name seemed to possess some faint meaning for Kaypack. Ignoring the money, he struggled to recall. "Radius," he said at last.

"Sung sent me."

"No," said Kaypack.

"Yes, sir, it's true. I—I'm supposed to give you this." Darcey indicated the money.

Veador stared in amazement. His astonishment was so great

that he hadn't yet had time to grow angry at Nova. Around him, the nervegun battle continued. One human and three aliens were dead. Veador simply waited for the moment when his commander would explain everything.

But Kaypack, oddly enough, appeared to be crying.

Finally, wiping his eyes with the back of a hand, Kaypack took the money from Darcey's outstretched palm and shoved it deep inside the outer pocket of his silversuit. He glanced at Veador, then at Nova, and took Darcey by the arm. "Come to my womb," he said. "We must talk in private."

"But, my commander," cried Veador, staggering forward to apologize.

Kaypack held up a hand. "Veador, I'll notify you when I need your services," he said evenly.

"Yes, my commander."

Kaypack led Darcey out of the room. The gunfight, fortunately, had ended. Veador looked across at Nova and suddenly began to grow very, very angry.

"Veador, no!" she cried.

Some of the children were growing impatient. One boy in the first row glared at me. "It sure is taking you a long time to get to the story."

"This is the story," I said.

"That's not what you said in the beginning. You said it was about the grayspace beast. Okay, so far we've got Kaypack, dumb Darcey, Nova, and an alien with a tail. Where's the beast?"

"I did warn you it was a long story," I gently remonstrated.

"I think you ought to leave more out," said a blond girl. "A good story—you taught us this yourself—is like a good egg. It has to be boiled down."

I was never adverse to intelligent criticism. "How about if I skip the next chapter, then?"

"What's that?" she asked me.

"Well, it's where Kaypack and Darcey meet. Darcey tells him about the beast, about his mission, about the ship."

"That's it?"

I nodded.

"Then skip it."

I shrugged. "All right, I will."

Resting alone in the soft pink core of his womb, Kail Kaypack struggled to remember exactly how it had been more than seven hundred common years previous when he and Darcey's parents had first reached the planet Radius.

The cruiser *Arjuna* had carried a full crew of ten experienced stellars on what was expected to be a routine exploratory mission. When the blue-green orb of Radius first appeared on the ship's four screens, Kaypack, as commander, experienced no strong emotion beyond the usual eager anticipation he felt when glimpsing a possibly inhabited world.

He recalled hurrying to the side of his chief alien specialist, a young woman named Nori Watt, who told him, "The nitrogen-oxygen balance is seventy-seven to twenty-two. Abundant plant life, obviously, on land and sea. Twenty-seven common-hour rotation. One tiny satellite."

"Intelligence?"

She shrugged. "No indications. Even from here, with advanced technology, something should appear."

"We'll go closer."

But closer—even planetary orbit—showed nothing more. Finally, Kaypack selected Nori and an assistant pilot, Sten Dawson, to accompany him below. Sten flew the shuttle.

They had barely penetrated the topmost layer of planetary clouds when communication with the orbiting *Arjuna* ceased.

"What the hell?" said Kaypack to Sten.

"I'm sorry, sir." Sten fiddled with the instruments. "I can't tell."

"Can you repair it?"

"I can't tell that, either."

Kaypack considered. "Then we'll go on. This should be only a short trip. Maybe you can correct the malfunction once we land."

"Yes, sir."

It wasn't till later that Kaypack learned the malfunction was caused by the abrupt death above of all seven remaining crew members.

From the air, they glimpsed traces of animal life, grim, lumbering beasts. Sten guided the shuttle past a jagged mountain range and turned toward the ocean shoreline. Kaypack directed him to land upon a bleak, barren stretch of coastal sand.

The three of them emerged from the bubble cockpit together. A line of evergreens rose past the edge of the sand. Sten Dawson took a step in that direction, grabbed hold of his chest, and keeled over.

Nori reached him first. She felt his arm and announced, "He's alive."

"Then get him back aboard the shuttle—hurry." He reached down to help her lift the unconscious man.

Nori noticed the alien first. Holding Sten's shoulders, she pointed toward the forest. "Kaypack, we've got company."

The alien was alone. He stood three meters off the ground and was generally humanoid in appearance. The alien's skin was colored a dull, lifeless shade of gray and he walked forward with a high, prancing step.

"Put him down," Kaypack ordered Nori.

As she lowered his body to the ground, Sten suddenly moaned.

Kaypack went forward, following the procedure he had used a dozen times before when contacting intelligent alien races. Holding both hands in the air, he bowed his head and repeated his name again and again.

The alien said, "My name is Sung and this is the planet Radius." He spoke common Galactic, though stiffly, enunciating unexpected syllables.

"You have known men before?" Kaypack instantly asked.

"We have long been aware of your existence."

Kaypack nodded, aware of the difference between what he had asked and what the alien—Sung—had replied. Of the dozen intelligent races he had discovered in the past, Kaypack considered only one more intelligent than humanity and none more technically advanced. "How?" he asked.

Sung seemed not to hear. He pointed at Sten, who had once more fallen unconscious. "Your companion suffers from a logabug. You must bring him to our village to be saved."

"I have a physician cube aboard my ship."

"That will not save him."

"How do I know you can do better?"

"You cannot depart."

"Are you threatening us?"

"Your ship is inoperative."

"You mean my shuttle?" Kaypack pointed behind. Nori cradled Sten's head in her lap and looked about with frightened wonder.

"That, and also the larger craft above. Both have been dispersed."

"My crew?" he cried.

"They have also been dispersed."

"You killed them!"

"No creature can really die."

"Don't give me that mumbo-jumbo. What are you? What kind of monster?"

"We have chosen to permit you three to live."

Kaypack squatted in the moist sand. Somehow his grief ebbed quickly. Even with the crew dead, he and these two lived on. That was what must concern him now. He remained firmly in command. "Tell me what you are."

"The natives of Radius. Elders of our race. There is no more to say." Sung knelt beside Kaypack.

In spite of the alien's words, Kaypack believed there was

much else to say. "But you want us to stay here—the three of us."

"You must."

"For how long?"

"That will be determined."

Kaypack fingered the butt of the nervegun he wore slung to his hip. "Another cruiser is certain to follow ours. We did not arrive here by random chance. Our intended route is known. When the *Arjuna* fails to return, we will be sought."

"Then other men will come to join you here."

"You can't imprison every stellar in the service."

"We have imprisoned no one."

Kaypack sensed the futility of further lies. Either Sung knew that the course followed by a grayspace explorer was indeed a matter of choice, dependent upon the peculiar circumstances of each voyage, or else he really did not care.

Kaypack went back to see Nori and Sten. "We're to carry him to their village. They can care for him there."

"Are you sure that's safe?"

"I don't see why not. They seem friendly enough."

"But he speaks Galactic. How can that be?"

Kaypack told the truth this time. "I'm afraid I don't have the slightest idea." Sten moaned softly. "Here, pick him up. Let's go now."

He had decided to wait a few days, until Sten was either better or dead, and then tell her about the crew and the ship.

The Radian village at first glance could have been any primitive settlement of mud-and-grass huts set down in a wide forest clearing. They were fed a light meal of cooked green leaves. Halfway through, Sten joined them. He remembered nothing of his brief illness. After he had eaten, Sten stood up and said to Kaypack, "I suppose we'll be going now, sir."

Kaypack showed his hesitation. "Going where?"

"Why, back to the shuttle, of course."

"The shuttle won't work," Kaypack said bleakly.

"Then we should notify the ship."

"The radio's broken, remember?"

"Well, I can fix that."

Kaypack looked away. "No, I don't think you can."

Nori—Kaypack believed she already guessed far more than he'd actually told her—said, "Kaypack, quit playing tag and just tell us. What is going on here?"

So he told them—about the *Arjuna*, its crew, what Sung had said. Oddly, though neither was pleased, both Nori and Sten accepted the news without despair. It was the planet, Kaypack decided. Radius was not a proper place for human grief.

The village held a population numbering close to five hundred. There were distinct male and female sexes but few children. Kaypack soon learned that the adults never spoke—not to one another or to their children. Sung alone occasionally conversed with the three stellars, but the other adult occupants of the village seemed barely aware of their presence. The children flocked around, excited and chattering, but Kaypack made little sense of their apparent language.

"I think they must be telepathic," Nori told Kaypack.

"No, that's impossible," he said. "Tests have shown that."

"For humans. For every other species we've found. These are Radians. Who has ever examined their brains? Removing a cruiser from planetary orbit ought to be impossible, too. You believe they did that."

"I have to."

"So why not telepathy, too?"

He shrugged bleakly. Why not indeed?

The gentle, idle existence he carved for himself soon grew boring. Until now, Kaypack had predicated his life upon an unending succession of unprecedented experience, but now no one day ever differed drastically from the one before. Nori and Sten grew accustomed to each other's company, but that left Kaypack even more alone than before.

In the third (apparent) month of their exile, Nori whispered that she was pregnant and expected to give birth.

"What sex?" Kaypack asked.

"Why? Do you care?"

"Not especially, just curious."

"Well, I can hardly find out here."

He glanced around the village—the grass and mud, the noisy children and silent adults. "No, I suppose not. But couldn't you have been more careful?"

"I doubt it, but why should I have tried?"

He indicated the surrounding village. "What child deserves to be born here? There's no way out."

She laughed at him. "Kaypack, don't you even know what this is?"

He shook his head. "What is it?"

"Paradise—what else? Look, no work, plenty of food, friendly company, total relaxation, beautiful scenery. Come out in the woods someday and look around. It's lovely."

"After an entire galaxy, I can't accept one thin woods. I think your paradise is boring. Besides, what about when we die?"

"You expect me to answer that?" She laughed again.

"I meant this child you're so eager to bear."

She shook her head in mock dismay. "Why should he die?"

"Not him, you. Me. Sten. Then what happens to the child?"

"What makes you think even we will die?"

"Name me somebody who doesn't."

"Sure. Sung."

Kaypack thought about that for a moment, then got to his feet. "I'm going for a walk in your woods," he said.

He had only gone a short distance when the village was swallowed up by encroaching foliage. A path opened before him and Kaypack decided to follow it until he grew hungry.

He passed a flat, glimmering pool of blue water and noticed, rising above, a line of green foothills. Behind and between these hills rose the gorgeous white peak of a genuine mountain. The well-worn trail led that way. Bunches of pink melon fruit dangled from frequent trees. After an hour or so, Kaypack sampled a bite. The fruit tasted sweet, and the meat proved unexpectedly filling. Kaypack walked many more hours, munching occasionally. He belched and spat out the flat dark seeds.

When night fell, Kaypack climbed a melon tree and rested within the fork of two main branches. He heard the patter of small animals scurrying upon the forest floor. Once, a large beast howled, some distance away. Kaypack ate a melon. His belly seemed full, threatening to bloat. He closed his eyes against the sensation and quickly dreamed.

Come morning, Kaypack considered returning to the village. His own stomach seemed round and pulsing with life. He decided to continue and walked all day in the direction of the white mountain. At nightfall, he ascended another melon tree, ate one fruit, and soon dreamed again.

On the third day of his journey, by which time he had entered the green foothills directly beneath the towering mountain, Kaypack discovered the body of a young boy nestled within a slim rock chasm a meter deep.

Crouching down, Kaypack turned the body so that he could see the boy's face. The eyes were open.

"Good God, what happened to you?" cried Kaypack. The front portion of the boy's body, especially his chest, was a mass of festering red welts. His skin was a patchwork of cuts and scratches.

"Gorgan." The boy seemed to understand what Kaypack had said, but, apparently recognizing him, fell silent.

"An animal?" asked Kaypack.

The boy said nothing but his eyes darted frantically—back in the direction of the white mountain. *Gorgan.* During his brief study of the native language, Kaypack had often heard the use of this term among the village children and has assumed it to be a consequential noun form. Could it be this mountain? He pointed toward the white summit and asked, "Gorgan?"

The boy looked fearfully about.

Reaching down, Kaypack tried to lift the boy in his arms, but the boy squirmed away in real terror and did not fall still until Kaypack drew back.

"You don't want my help, I assume."

The boy nodded, big-eyed like a human child.

"You may die out here. If you're from the same village I am, it's three days' walk. You'll never make it."

If the boy understood, he gave no sign. Kaypack stepped toward him. The boy scurried away, flopping down the length of the chasm.

Kaypack drew up short. "All right, but I want you to know"—he waved in front of him—"I'm going up that mountain. I'm going to climb Gorgan Mount."

The boy understood. The look in his eyes—fear, anger, rage, and disgust—proved that. He had easily forgotten his physical pain. Kaypack understood that he was, no doubt, about to violate some local prerogative. In the past he would not have considered committing such an act but in the past he had never been kept prisoner or had seven of his crew murdered.

"I'm going," Kaypack told the Radian boy that day.

He could no longer recall whether it took two or three additional days to reach the actual summit of the white mountain. In either event, the arrival itself was a moment he could not forget. Hauling his body, torn and wounded, those final cold meters . . .

On Gorgan Mount, Kaypack discovered why some Radians talked while others did not.

He turned back down the mountain refreshed and enlightened. He sought out Sung in the village below and demanded his personal freedom. "I want to go home," he said, "and there's no way you can keep me anymore."

Sung said, "You are an elder."

While saying this, Sung never opened his mouth nor uttered a sound.

These were among the events of Kaypack's long life that he would never neglect. It was the perfect detail—the scent of the air, the touch of wind upon flesh, the accent of a spoken voice—that he strained to recall exactly.

Darcey popped through the entrance tube and bounded softly across the squirmy floor.

"Did you sleep well?" Kaypack asked, banishing Radius for another time.

"Oh, sure," said Darcey, who had spent the last hours in Veador's adjoining womb. "I wanted to know if there was anything else you wanted to ask me before we left."

"Well, as a matter of fact . . ." Kaypack decided not to disillusion Darcey right away: leaving would neither be so easy nor so soon. "Did you ever climb that big mountain back on Radius?"

"You mean Gorgan Mount." Darcey showed surprise and his face further reflected some deep humiliation. "The elders said it was forbidden, sir."

Kaypack didn't want to hurt the boy, yet he believed this was knowledge that should be shared. "When I lived there with your parents, I climbed it."

"The elders let you?" Darcey nearly sprang to his feet in agitation.

"No, no." Kaypack drew him down. "Don't think that. I snuck up there. I went even before I knew what it was. When Sung found out about it, he showed some real emotion —I think it was the only time—he was pissed as hell."

"What did you find there?" Darcey asked.

"Do you want to know? It is forbidden."

Darcey showed the strain between transitional loyalties. He opted for Kaypack. "Yes."

"Then I just wish I was capable of telling you. The problem is, it's the spirit of the planet that resides on that mountaintop. I don't just mean the elders, the people, but the whole damn planet, oceans and trees and specks of dirt. See? I told you that wouldn't make sense, and I suppose it doesn't."

"In a way it does."

"Sure, but your situation was completely different from mine. You wanted to stay on Radius and be an elder, while I wanted nothing except to get home. Your mother used to tell me it was a paradise, but for me paradise isn't sitting on your tail, it's being busy with something supremely important every waking minute and doing a hell of job with that something to the best of your ability. So, when I was an elder, the first thing I did was tell Sung I wanted to go home. He had to let me. There was a scancircle in the woods. It was the first I'd ever seen myself. Sung used it to send me back to the human galaxy."

"Just you?"

Kaypack nodded tightly. This was the part he wanted to be sure Darcey understood.

"Mother and Father couldn't go, too?"

"No, they could have. I was an elder—remember? If I'd demanded it, they'd have gone."

"Then why—?"

"They didn't want to. Remember? She said it was paradise. What I want to know is, do you feel the same way, because —if you do—I think you should stay here. What the elders want of me—the grayspace beast—I don't think anyone should go out there unless they really believe in it."

"No, I do believe in it—I really do."

"You wanted to come here?"

"Not at first, no—I admit that. But after Mother died, after I saw how lonely it was going to be, then I wanted off. And I like it here—it's so alive. Radius was like . . . what are these places called where they lay the dead?"

"A tomb? A mausoleum?"

"Yes. Radius was like that."

"Space is different, too. Especially grayspace."

"But I'm ready for it, sir."

"Good." Kaypack reached out and punched Darcey's shoulder. "Then I'm ready for you, too, boy."

Shortly afterward, Veador popped down the entrance tube. His tail twitched with frantic agitation and Kaypack could see that he was upset. "Veador, what is it?" he asked.

"Treachery has been committed against us, my commander. That dreadful woman. She has revealed all."

Kaypack felt more amusement than concern. "She doesn't know all."

"But she knows about the money—his money." Veador meant Darcey. "And she has told Rickard Welch."

"In return for the usual reward?"

"I would assume so, my commander," said Veador, a desolate expression upon his face.

"Then that is a problem—a minor one, but a problem. Nova has told the authorities about us," Kaypack told Darcey. He pulled on his lip in a vivid depiction of deep thought. "Here," he said to Veador, removing the wad of money Darcey had given him and transferring the top four bills to Veador's hand, "I want you to take this and hire me a crew. Find me four good people—a navigator, a pilot, and two alien specialists."

"There are no such people as these upon Paradise Planet, my commander. Or anywhere. Those are grayspace positions."

"I know that, Veador."

"But, my commander, what do we need with such a crew? We don't own any ship, especially not a grayspace one."

"Ah, but we do now, Veador." Kaypack could not conceal his glee. "That is what Darcey here has brought us."

"A grayspace ship?"

Kaypack nodded firmly.

Veador failed to relax. "But the danger to us stands immediate, my commander. Perhaps I have not made myself sufficiently clear. Rickard Welch. If he finds you or me in possession of such large funds, the money will be confiscated. I think—I believe—I suggest we should voluntarily settle our syndicate debt before charges are laid against us."

"Oh, bull, Veador." Kaypack laughed aloud. Winking at Darcey, he said, "We need that money for our hunting trip."

"Hunting?" Veador showed his bewilderment. "My commander, Paradise Planet is devoid of wildlife."

"That's true," said Kaypack, with a thoughtful nod, "but grayspace is different. We're going to use this money to go beast hunting. Now, come on." Kaypack moved toward the exit chute. "I've got to go hide out for a time, and I think I know the perfect place."

"But, my commander—" Veador went nipping at his heels.

"Darcey, you come, too," said Kaypack, as he leaped head first through the chute hole.

"I think that's a lousy copout," said one of the boys.

"What?" I asked surprised. "Veador? Nova? Kaypack? Who did what?"

"Neither. You. Kaypack found the spirit of Radius high on Gorgan Mount. It wasn't just the people—it was specks of dirt, too. What kind of dumb story is that? You cut off the narrative before he gets there and then later you toss off that cheap crap and call it a description."

"Well, it's true," I said defensively.

"And a copout. Even if you are Kaypack. A lousy copout."

"No—think. Since you came to this school—this goes for all of you—how many descriptions of transcendental experience have you heard or read?"

"About half a million and five," said the boy.

"And each of you—if you were novitiates, you wouldn't be here—has no doubt suffered some sort of experience also. How many of these have made sense? What you read or what you felt? Brahman equals Atman. God is Love. Even the oldest, most simple mystical expressions truly say nothing."

"At least they try."

"No," I said. "By not trying, what I'm doing is leaving it up to each of you to decide. Use your own experience—whether you can describe it or not—whether it makes sense or not—use it. What happened to Kail Kaypack on Gorgan Mount was a mighty thing."

"You ought to know, my commander," said that first boy again.

"Shut up—he's Darcey," said a girl.

"Or Nova." Laughter.

"Or Veador." Giggles.

I waited for them to subside, then said, "What happened to Kaypack on the mountain deeply affected his later life. Find some experience of your own similar to that and transfer the emotions you felt to what happened to Kaypack at the time. I think that's as close as you can come to understanding what he discovered. Anything I could tell you in the way of description would be redundant."

"Your story's still going no place," said a girl, one of my best students. She spoke with sorrow. "Nothing's happened yet at all."

"Well, something soon will," I promised. "This is the end of the first segment. The second is more direct and action-filled."

"The beast gobbles up Kaypack?" said a boy.

"Oh, we haven't come to the beast yet," I said. And quickly, before their moans and groans could drown me out, I began to cough like a baying mule.

TWO

"Now," I said, "where were we?"

"The crew," prodded a girl.

"Yes, right. Now, in the old days, an average-sized crew for a grayspace cruiser usually numbered nine or ten. There would be a commander, first officer, engineer, pilot, crew chief, one or two alien specialists, navigator, and serf. This meant that Veador, under instructions from Kaypack, would have to seek out and hire as many as seven additional—"

"Wait a minute," said a boy, holding up a hand. "Does this mean we're going to have some new characters?"

"Well, yes, a few," I said. "The story's still barely started yet, so there's still plenty of room for development. They aren't just spear carriers, if that's what you mean."

"No, I mean, is one of them going to be you?"

With a sigh, I tried to show the proper amount of irritation. "What is this fascination of yours with trying to identify me with one of the characters? What if I say I'm Johann Helsing? Will that satisfy you?"

"Not unless it's true."

"Oh, shut up," I finally said.

"If you insist."

"Mr. Helsing," added a voice from the back.

Johann Helsing sat poised upon the edge of the chair, his nervous little fists twitching upon the tabletop as he struggled to meet the demanding gaze of the green-skinned, long-tailed alien across from him. He recognized the creature as a member of the Mayan breed. "What makes you believe I would even consider such a ridiculous proposition?" Helsing removed his old-style spectacles and scrubbed the lenses thoroughly with a sterile cloth. "I'm a mathematician, not a . . . a . . . spaceman."

"I came to you," said the alien (Veador, of course), "just for that reason. There are no spacemen anymore, sir, but there are mathematicians. My commander seeks the services of one capable of computing grayspace charts. Of all the men on Paradise Planet, my researches indicate you are the only one qualified."

Helsing, who enjoyed praise enormously because he so seldom received any of it (computing gambling odds for a sharpie syndicate was not a proud profession, in spite of its complexities), preened himself and smiled. "None of the other oddsmakers in the same class as me?"

"Hardly, sir," said Veador.

"Oh, I could have told you that myself," said Helsing.

"It would be a privilege to serve with you on a crew. I'm sure the others feel the same."

Helsing squinted and hurriedly replaced his spectacles. "Others? What others? You mean I'm not the first you've asked?" He raised his voice in spite of knowing that this office—his own—was hardly safe from syndicate eavesdropping.

Veador spoke more softly. "The first navigator, of course. But the crew is filling up fast. Not surprisingly. You must understand this is the first grayspace expedition in nearly three hundred years. Many will leap at the chance to be part of this historic event."

Helsing believed fervently in history. "But the syndicate disapproves and the syndicate pays my salary. One that exceeds—need I emphasize this point?—the tiny retainer you have so kindly offered me."

"The syndicate fears my commander."

Helsing let his amazement show. In twenty common-years' laboring in this office, he had never gone a minute without fearing the syndicate. "Whatever for? The syndicate is rich, powerful, strong. Kaypack is—at least others say so—a crank."

"A visionary. The syndicate is complacent."

"That's all?"

Veador stood and loomed above the shriveled man (Helsing) at the desk. Helsing had been born small and had grown little in the fifty years since. Veador said, "My commander feels it is enough. Three hundred years ago, the syndicate and other rulers of the human galaxy shut down the Grayspace Stellar Service in favor of scansystem travel. Planetary exploration thus ceased. My commander believes our current mission will prove extraordinarily successful. Human history will be transformed and a new war of galactic expansion begun. My commander believes the syndicate fears him because they sense in his vision the seeds of their own extinction."

Helsing felt like laughing at these silly pretensions but another voice told him no. What was he, after all? A mathematician, that was what, a talent born in the blood. He loved numbers, loved the concrete abstractions of a second and superior universe. When he worked with his figures—even when he merely calculated the odds for some new gambling device—he entered a distinct realm far removed from the jagged realities that surrounded him here.

What could it be like out there in space, grayspace? What huge figures would be his to control? An entire galaxy of numbers, thousands upon thousands of them. His eyes suddenly moistened at the thought of such beauty, and he hastily removed his spectacles to hide the emotion. "I—I—" he said with difficulty. "I'd like to think it over."

But Veador, who had possibly seen far more than he now admitted, shook his big head. "I must ask for your decision now."

"It could cost me my job," said Helsing.

"Either way, I'm sure it will," said Veador.

"Then I—"

"Four," said a loud boy.

"What?" I looked up.

"I was counting the crew. Kaypack, Darcey, Veador, and now this Helsing guy. That's four."

"But who said Helsing even accepted?"

The boy laughed. "Look, would you waste all that time describing the conversation, telling us about the guy's old-style spectacles and how he was born small if, in the end, he was going to tell Veador to take a hike?"

I had to smile. "I guess not."

"I told you to be subtle. Now skip the dumb punchline and get on with the rest of it."

"Get ready for five," I said, subtly.

Maria Novitsky, broad brown face contorted by rage, reached out desperately as the lithe, green-skinned alien slid past her. With a final effort, Maria managed to fasten a tight grip upon the alien's trailing tail. Holding on, she refused to budge as the alien (Veador again) screamed and yelped.

"Stand still!" she snapped, ignoring the crowd of fleecies who turned to stare in horror. "Damn it, I've got you now, so give up."

It was clear from Veador's expression that he had no intention of surrendering without a fight. He kicked, clawed, leaped, squirmed, quivered, sprang, wiggled, barked, wept.

"I'm not letting you go," Maria said, between her teeth. "Not till you tell me what I want to know."

Seeing the hopelessness of struggle, Veador at last subsided. He tried to plead. "I am engaged upon a mission of supreme importance for my commander."

"Don't bleat," said Maria, snorting. She held tight to Veador's tail. "If I tear this off, it's all the same to me. I know about your mission. It's what I want to talk about."

A desperate look entered Veador's eyes. He stood trapped upon the central midway, not far from Maria's neon place of business. Two security agents, who had followed Veador most of the day, stood near. Neither made an effort to interfere.

"Release me," said Veador.

"I want a job," said Maria. "On your crew."

"Impossible."

"Then I'll break off your tail and make you eat it." She started to twist. When the panic in Veador's eyes spread to cover his face, she let go. "Now that's better," she said, poised to spring at any moment. The fleecies no longer stared. Weird happenings were ten-a-minute on Paradise Planet; you could stare all day. "I know you're gathering a crew for Kaypack and I want to sign up."

Veador shook his head. "Impossible." Maria moved for his tail. "All the crew slots are filled," he said hastily.

"Bull on that. I happen to know you've approached twenty-seven people today and the only one who said yes was little Johann Helsing, who probably went loony all of a sudden. That leaves plenty of room for me."

Veador opened his mouth too wide. "How do you know of this? I directed Helsing to say nothing."

"Who said he did? I have my ways. Now either sign me up or else I'll go see Kaypack personally."

Veador smiled smugly. "My commander has gone into hiding."

Maria's expression matched the alien's. "And I know where," she lied.

"You do not—no one does."

"I knew about Helsing, didn't I?"

She saw that she'd thrown him one and waited a moment for the rage to pass from his face.

She said, "Look, Veador, I know you don't approve of me and I know why. You think I've corrupted Kaypack since he's been here. Well, that isn't true. He was corrupt a long time before he ever set foot in my establishment."

"You are deceitful," said Veador.

"You mean because my helpmates are not real?"

"You make metal creatures and call them women. People think they have found enormous beauty when it is really a lie."

Maria was surprised. She had never know that aliens could be so sensitive. "Not people," she said. "Fleecies. That's what we're here for. To fleece."

"Not my commander."

"Your commander knows my girls are robots." As she said this, she saw from his expression that this was really the crux of his dislike of her, and she further realized that there was nothing she could do about it. "Look," she said, raising her voice to a pitch that the two security agents could not help overhearing, "I want on your crew and I won't take no for an answer. I know as well as Kaypack that there's money to be made out there hand-over-fist. I'm sick of this place. I hate those robots as much as anyone. I want off Paradise Planet and I want to be rich. You're offering me a chance to have both. Now hire me."

"Never," said Veador, unrelenting.

She grabbed for his tail and kept her voice at the same level. "Then I'm going to see Kaypack. Right now. I'm going straight there."

Veador saw the security agents, too. He calculated quickly —Maria watched the sadness spread in his eyes. "You are lying," he said.

"You'll never know."

"Five," said the same boy.

I nodded. "Five."

"I don't like her," said another.

"She's not as bad as she sounds at first. Remember, Veador

is prejudiced—all of us are. He wants to blame Maria for Kaypack's own weaknesses."

"What weaknesses?" asked a younger girl, who—in her innocence—make no effort to conceal her confusion.

"I don't think I should go into that now," I said.

"He's being subtle," said a boy.

"It's a euphemism," said a girl, who was perhaps closer to graduation than anyone else in the class.

"Well, I don't like it," said the original questioner.

"Neither do I," I admitted, "but it can be fun, too. If you understand what I mean, then fine, and if you don't, then it'll be something for you to wonder about as you grow older, and wondering never hurt anybody."

"I wonder what he means," said a boy.

"I wonder if he's one of Maria's helpmates," said another.

At the end of the day, as artificial evening crept upon the midway like a nocturnal bird of prey, Veador gazed bleakly at two of the five fingers of his right hand. That was the grand total: two crew members. Johann Helsing, Maria Novitsky. During the course of the day he had approached several dozen others. Five had cursed him out, one had attacked him physically, another had spat, two had laughed, one had snorted, and the rest had merely said no.

Commander Kail Kaypack, secure in his hiding place, awaited Veador's glorious return. How could he (Veador) tell his commander the terrible truth? The human race—Kaypack's own people—no longer desired to go journeying outward. Promises of adventure and excitement, even profit, no longer bore any real meaning for these beings. Except for Helsing, Veador had been unable to pander to their deepest desires. Was it even possible to seduce complacency? Poor Kaypack. Veador wished his duty did not encompass bringing grief to his commander. Kaypack stood beyond disillusionment. In spite of eight hundred years of existence, Kaypack remained a romantic, quick to expect and accept the sudden best in human nature. His vision never cleared to the point where warped, peeling reality peeped through.

"Sir Veador?" said a strange, lilting voice.

Veador looked up and saw, arm in arm, a matching pair of native Simerians. The race was a rare one, seldom seen beyond the limits of their one home planet. Both naked, the Simerians showed narrow blank eyes within the folds of their ghostly pale faces. Were they male or female? Even nude, it was impossible to tell.

"How do you know my name?" he asked. Veador had found a shadowy place on the midway not far from the defunct grayspace concession; he had not expected to be disturbed.

"We have come to serve Kaypack." The two spoke as one —it was part of their way. One Simerian or another, they were truly all the same.

"Kaypack has been to your world." Veador recalled that Kaypack had originally discovered Simeria some seven hundred years before.

"We saw him briefly."

Were they claiming to be that old? Veador wondered, then suddenly realized he did not care one way or the other. "Go away. Kaypack is in hiding. No one knows where he is."

"But we wish to join his crew."

Veador groaned. "Not you, too. Is there anyone on this planet who doesn't know?"

"Oh, we knew about the crew long before we ever came here."

"Yes. Of course." Veador's past contact with Simerians had taught him that the galaxy failed to contain their equals when it came to lying.

"And we have much past experience. We have served in various positions aboard many past cruisers. Also, nine times we have seen the grayspace beast and have twice felt its aspect."

Veador shivered at the mention of the beast. Among all of

Kaypack's stories, it was his least favorite. Reaching into a pocket of the narrow apron he wore, he drew out the remaining two bills Kaypack had given him. He gazed bleakly at the Simerians. The thought of months cooped up aboard a single ship with these two things disgusted him. But, was there really any real chance of that? Was this scheme ever apt to be transformed from dream to reality?

As the sky turned suddenly black and the first pinprick stars twinkled through, Veador decided no. He handed the Simerians one bill each. "You're hired," he said. "When we need you, we'll call you."

"You may find us here." The two stood stiff and still, as if intending to remain indefinitely rooted in the sawdust beneath their feet.

Veador no longer cared. With the money now exhausted, he was eager only to get back to Kaypack and tell him the news. Should he mention the identities of these last two? That they were merely crazy Simerians? Perhaps Kaypack would not think to ask.

When he passed the two security agents who continued to follow him everywhere, Veador saw that they were giggling. Even among humans, Simerians were regarded with deep contempt. Suddenly, in a fit of cold premonition, Veador envisioned the crew he was signing. There was young Darcey, shriveled Helsing, amoral Novitsky, mad Simerians, Kail Kaypack, and himself. The seven of us, he thought, and the wastes of grayspace. Shivering with fear, Veador quickly squelched the terrible vision. The two agents pursued him along the broad midway. Veador walked parallel to the main casino. Suddenly, without warning, he dropped his tail to the sawdust, then used it to propel himself straight up into the air like a rising rocket. The agents stood with gaping mouths as Veador hit with practiced ease the round wide opening of a casino entrance tube. Once inside, he rose swiftly to the top floor. Disembarking, he counted slowly to ten. He dived for the nearest exit chute. Outside again, neither agent could be seen. Veador smiled, his first happiness of the day. As always, surprise had overwhelmed any stray intelligence. Scattering fleecies, Veador turned and darted away.

"Seven," said a girl.

"Six," I corrected.

"Huh?" She showed me her fingers. "Kaypack, Veador, Darcey, Helsing, Novitsky, two Simerians. That's seven."

"It's six. Two Simerians, three Simerians, fifty thousand three hundred forty-nine Simerians: it's always just one."

"I don't get it."

"That's why you ought to listen to the rest of the story."

When Veador reached his commander's hiding place, he found Kaypack seated with Darcey on the squishy floor of the tiny womb. Nova, bound and gagged, lay behind them. "She tried to scream," Kaypack explained. "It was the best way of silencing her."

"Well, it is her womb," said Darcey.

Veador glared, unsympathetic. "She performed treachery against my commander."

A moment later, Rickard Welch, chief security agent for the Paradise Planet Syndicate, came toppling through the entrance tube. Striking the soft floor, he bounced twice like a bloated rubber ball.

Veador leaped to his feet, cracking his head against the low ceiling. "You have followed me here," he cried, desperately ashamed. "I have failed my commander."

"Shut up and sit down, alien," said Welch. He situated his round body in a comfortable sitting position and pointed a plump finger at Kaypack, who now faced him. "I've come to join you, not arrest you. If the syndicate bosses knew I was here—knew that I knew where you were—it'd be my head, too."

"You followed Veador?" said Kaypack. He spoke calmly.

Even Welch's dramatic entrance had failed to ruffle him. As ever, Veador loved and admired his commander.

"No need. It was damn obvious, frankly. Where else would you go? Everything's monitored except a few cheap wombs. Nobody would be apt to hide you. Nova screwed you, so you'd want to screw her back. Ergo . . ."

"This is Darcey," Kaypack said, pointing. "The rest of us you know."

"I know Darcey, too," said Welch. He stared at the boy with open interest. His tiny eyes grew as large as buttons.

"Nova?" asked Kaypack.

"Yes, and monitoring. We check the scansystem for every new arrival. This boy came from a hole in the middle of empty space. Obviously, we were curious. Where'd he get the money?"

Kaypack reached into his silversuit pocket. "First you accept a bill, then I'll talk."

"I said I wanted to join you."

"Make it official." Kaypack held out the bill.

"If you wish." Welch tucked the money away.

"Now tell me what's on your mind. We're going into grayspace. I have a ship—an old cruiser of mine, the *Arjuna*. Darcey has brought us sufficient funds to scan a crew."

"You have a co-ordinate?" Welch asked, surprised.

"I've been given one."

"By whom?"

"I'll tell you that later. Right now I want to know what you're thinking."

"A fair question," said Welch. "I suppose I shouldn't expect you to trust me."

Veador spoke this time: "No."

"It began with Nova," said Welch. "She came to me, said you had some money, wouldn't pay your debt. I started routine action, filed a report. Today this grayspace stuff started coming in. I filed another report. The syndicate hit the dome.

I got calls and calls. They wanted you dead. Assassination wasn't only recommended, it was demanded."

Kaypack showed no emotion at the closeness of death. "So you wondered why."

"Obviously. You were a crackpot, a crank. I thought so—the syndicate didn't. I got to thinking, what if they were right? You went into grayspace, so what? Money, I decided, and power. Thousands of virgin worlds out there. What could happen? A whole new era of exploitation. Scarce resources—scarce no longer. Who holds the strings on the moneybag? The man who's got it in his hand. I want to be that man."

"On my crew?"

"Exactly."

Veador wanted to protest. His commander was an idealist, not an exploiter.

Kaypack spoke first. "Then you're hired. Now I need your help."

Welch grinned. "I thought you would."

"We have to get off Paradise Planet."

"There's only one way."

"You're willing to try it?"

Welch nodded. "I've already talked to Maria Novitsky. Between us—especially with Helsing, too—it can be done."

"What can be done?" Darcey asked, unafraid to display his ignorance and confusion.

"In order for us to escape this world," said Kaypack, "we have to make it so that nobody cares. The only way to do that is to create such a mess that nobody will notice. Mr. Welch knows how to create that mess."

"I've been thinking about it for twenty years," Welch admitted.

Darcey sat with Kaypack. Gagged to silence, Nova slept behind them. Darcey said, "Sir, why haven't you told them about the grayspace beast?"

"Because I'd rather be a liar than a fool. If they knew about the beast, how many do you think would have said yes?"

"Veador."

Kaypack smiled. "That's one."

"But, sir," said Darcey, "aren't you going to have to tell them sometime? Mr. Welch thinks he's going to be rich. The beast won't do that for him, will it?"

"They don't believe in the beast, Darcey."

"But you've seen it."

Kaypack nodded firmly. "There is a beast, Darcey—I have often seen it with my own good eyes. The beast dwells in the gray universe, the place where no living thing can exist, the cosmic wastes. Who has not heard tell of the stellar crew emerging mad to a man from the gray wastes and bearing a lunatic tale of a silver glittering creature as large as a small moon? Aye, Darcey, I have seen the grayspace beast and I know that it is evil." In spite of the intensity of his words, Kaypack put little feeling behind them.

"But, sir," said Darcey, "what exactly is the beast?"

Kaypack shook his head. "I don't know."

"But you can kill it?"

"I don't know that, either."

"The elders think you can."

"Do they?" Kaypack smiled. "Or is it that they hope I can? Hush." He pointed at Nova. "I think she's waking up."

"Foul!"

"Cheat!"

"Foul!"

I looked up, innocent as the baby lamb. "What do you mean?"

"That was no conversation," said a spokesman. "They didn't say one thing we didn't already know, and Kaypack's longest speech was nothing but a word-for-word replay of exactly what he told Veador back in chapter one."

"So?"

"So you cheated us. You promised us the beast and gave us old beans."

"Then I suggest you think about the significance of those old beans," I said haughtily, enjoying myself to the hilt and beyond.

"There is none," the boy said flatly.

I tilted an eyebrow. "You should know something now about Kaypack and the beast that you didn't know before."

"What?" Bluntly.

"Why, that Kaypack never set eyes on the beast in his life," I said. Bluntly.

The excitement and tension flowed so strongly through the tiny cramped womb that Darcey twitched as he sat, clenched and unclenched his fists, trembled, and felt his mouth and tongue run dry. The entire crew of the *Arjuna* had gathered in this one location. In counterclockwise rotation sat Darcey, Veador, Johann Helsing, the Simerians, Nova, Rickard Welch, and Maria Novitsky. As commander, Kail Kaypack squatted in the privileged center of the tightly drawn circle. His long legs, neatly folded, nearly touched those of most others.

"Rickard," said Kaypack, "suppose you discuss your ideas now that all of us are present."

"Well, I believe it's pretty damn obvious," said Welch. "The only sane way of getting us off this planet is to keep the rest of them so busy they don't notice us slipping away."

"The scancircle is guarded," Maria put in. "I went there this morning. The agents are damn inconspicuous—like a bird's beak on a human face."

"They have no need to be subtle," Welch said. "Neither do we. I'm talking about a huge, raging conflagration that will take ten times the men they have to control."

"You have a way of arranging that?" asked Maria.

"I do."

"There are only nine of us."

"Eight," said Nova.

"Only three are crucial to my plan. Johann, what's the most essential industry on Paradise Planet?"

Helsing jumped at the mention of his name. His hands shook; his spectacles balanced precariously at the tip of his moist, sweating nose. "Gambling, of course. The casinos."

"See?" said Welch to Maria. "And Johann establishes the odds. Tomorrow, suppose he gives them a gentle fudge."

"Oh, no—oh, no," said Helsing, horrified. "If I ever tried to do that—even an infinitesimal little bit—I'd lose my job for sure."

Welch glared. "Whether you do or not, you'll lose your life. I've seen the order, man. The syndicate calls you a traitor. If they weren't fishing for Kaypack, you'd be atoms now."

"But I haven't done anything," Helsing said.

"We fudge the odds just enough to plop the advantage into the fleecie's lap. What happens then?"

"The casino would shut down," said Helsing, who had recovered somewhat from his previous horror.

"Shut the doors on a few thousand angry fleecies and they'll tear the place apart, I'll tell you that. Then there's Maria. She can do her part simply doubling her fees. Let the fleecie have his fun—then charge him. What's worse, let him know they're robots." Welch giggled into a fist. "If that doesn't cause a riot, then I'm the maddest hatter in the room."

"You said three," said Maria.

"Myself. The divisionary possibilities in my line of work are immense. Especially since they trust me. Take that fake sky we all know so dearly. Suppose I grab the controls and give it a shake. Make daytime midnight and vice versa. It'll disorient people, drive them batty. I activate a disembodied voice, which proceeds to announce impending doom. Paradise Planet has slipped out of orbit and is plunging like a leaden ball toward the mother world beneath. Now you tell me. Coupled with the rest, is that enough to cause a blowup?"

"People will get hurt," Kaypack said hesitantly.

"People will die," Veador said. "Hundreds of them."

"Then tell me a better way," said Welch, his eyes glowing with fierce pride. "And the rest of you can help. The Simerians are enough to scare people by themselves. Veador is an obnoxious sight, too. Darcey and Nova—"

"Not me," interrupted Nova.

"—can stir up a little trouble. When the doom message rings down, panic. Scream, howl, shout. Panic is contagious— it's a disease of the flesh in its way. At the peak of the mess, we converge on the scancircle. A few minutes later, we're aboard the *Arjuna* and on our way to riches."

Maria smiled lightly. "I really think it'll work."

"We won't be able to bring supplies," Kaypack said doubtfully. "No food or water."

"It can't be helped," Welch said. "We'll have to make do with what's aboard. Johann—" Welch turned. "How long will it take you to stack the odds? When's the soonest you can be ready?"

Helsing showed no sign of eagerness. "In a week, two—"

"I'll give you three days," Welch said.

Helsing nodded, a barely discernible gesture.

"Splendid," said Welch, applauding himself. "Damn splendid indeed."

"I hope you're right," said Kaypack.

After the meeting concluded, most members of the crew departed one at a time. At last only Veador, Nova, Kaypack, and Darcey remained within the abruptly spacious womb. Kaypack turned to Darcey and said, "Why don't you and Nova go for a walk?"

"You don't trust me," said Nova, glaring. "I'll go straight for an agent and spill the works."

Kaypack seemed disinterested. Darcey, who had spent most of his recent time alone in Veador's dank womb, welcomed the opportunity to step freely. "Come on," he urged. "I'll keep watch on you."

"As if you could stop me from doing anything," Nova said.

"You're part of the crew now," said Darcey.

"That's his crazy idea." She meant Kaypack. "I never agreed to anything."

"Nova, go with Darcey," Kaypack said. "It'll do you both some good."

"And it'll ruin you." She sprang up angrily and jerked a thumb toward the exit chute. "Come on, stupid," she told Darcey. "If he wants to be crazy, that's his right."

Outside, it was nighttime. Because of the sudden, swift transformations of the sky, Darcey still had trouble recalling when it was night or day. The stars were presently winking. He counted four small visible moons drifting past. The midway surged as great waves of sharpies and fleecies swept past.

"Let's go somewhere else," Nova said. "I'm sick to death of seeing people."

Darcey didn't mention that she'd seen almost no one during the past few days. He often kept silent with her, avoiding the obvious. Of all the creatures he had met here, human and otherwise, she puzzled him the most deeply. That first night, she had fooled him. No one had ever done that before. He had to wonder which was the disguise. Who was the real Nova?

"This way." She pointed between adjoining concessions, a narrow passage like a roofless tunnel. "At least it'll be empty back here."

"Would you tell me something?" Darcey said as they edged through the shadows. Through thin walls, giggling fleecies could be heard.

"I doubt it."

"Why don't you want to be in the crew? Do you like it here that much?"

"Compared to what? A spaceship full of crazies?"

"I'm not crazy, am I?"

"Probably—but Kaypack is enough. Why don't you talk to him? He seems sure enough I'm already signed on board."

"You took the money he gave you."

"I always take the money people give me."

"Are you afraid?"

"No." She was angry again. Darcey sensed that he should have kept silent.

They emerged from the passageway in a dark, empty, almost mysterious place, where the sawdust lay still and the concessions were silent. Nova dropped suddenly to the ground. "This is the part they shut down last year. Business has been sour."

Darcey sat beside her. Only the fake stars in the violet sky provided real illumination. He saw her face but not the expression. "I think you really do want to go with us, but you don't want to show you're excited. That way, if it doesn't work, you won't be disappointed."

"No, I'll be killed. Why do you think Kaypack trusts me enough to let me run loose? He gave me that money. I'm part of the plot now. If you go, I go."

"You didn't have to take it."

She sighed. "I suppose not. Habits are hard to break."

He attempted to explain his real feelings to her. "You're a lot different from the others. In many ways, you're more like me than them."

"Bull," she said.

"No, it's true. I think we both want the same things."

"You want money?"

"No, that's Welch. And that Maria woman. Not us."

"Speak for yourself."

Two fleecies, deeply intoxicated, stumbled past, arm in arm. Darcey discovered a mournful and reassuring tedium in their slow, ambling walk. Alone, each would have fallen flat. Together, they not only stood, they moved.

"To find answers," he said. "That's what we want.

Kaypack, too, but especially us. It's a human drive. Even Welch and Maria have some of it. And the syndicate. They want to know the answers but they're afraid to face them. That's why we're in the crew. We're not afraid."

"I told you I wasn't."

Inspired perhaps by the surrounding silence, Darcey impulsively gripped Nova's hand. She responded, and although he couldn't see her mouth, he smiled at her in delight. "I'm glad you're coming with us."

He heard her mocking laughter. "You are weird. Darcey," she said passionately, "you are the weirdest person I've ever known. What makes you go beep-beep? It's not the same as the rest of us."

"I told you about my life on Radius."

"Sure, and that was crazy enough. But this is a different kind of craziness. You seem to stare right through people. Do you know what an X-ray is, Darcey? That's you—the X-ray man."

"I think they trained me."

"Who? The people on that planet?"

Darcey nodded. It was hard to remember the darkness and necessity to speak with words alone. "Kaypack says that's why the concession didn't fool me. I was trained to see through illusion. I guess it's the same with people."

"How?"

He shrugged. "I really don't remember."

"Then are you sure it's real? I like you, Darcey, but right now you're talking like you caught Kaypack's disease."

"What's that?"

"A messiah complex. You believe you've been sent to save the universe, and every step you take is riddled with supreme significance. That's plain bull, Darcey. We're all warts on God's behind."

"Well, there is something," he said hesitantly.

"Something else?"

He nodded, feeling her hand on his. He knew that the tension he felt had reached her. "Have you ever heard of the grayspace beast?"

She released his hand in apparent relief. "Sure, it's a legendary monster. Kaypack works it into his concession sometimes."

"Well, we're going to kill it," he said. "That's our . . . our task."

While Darcey slept in Veador's dank womb, his dreams were frequently tormented by false memories of his past home. With Gorgan Mount looming tall ahead of him, he marched relentlessly forward. His body was naked, the sun blistering-hot, and Sung, at his shoulder, said, "We have provided you this chance to show that you are worthy. You must not fail. You claim you are our equal—now prove it—prove it."

"But I can't—I want—" Darcey struggled to speak past his swollen tongue. "It keeps moving."

"No," said Sung, "you are the miserable thing that is failing."

Darcey's eyes filled with tears of shame. He walked faster and faster—ignoring the pain of his bleeding feet—but the mountain never came closer. He had already walked for many days and now believed that some great beast lay hidden beyond the edge of the horizon. Whenever Darcey managed to approach the sacred mountain, the beast reached out with huge, violent paws and caught hold of the scruff of the land, drawing the mountain and everything with it farther and farther away. Yet, still, Darcey marched on.

"I have seen a thousand children climb that mountain," said Sung. "True, many have failed, but they were unworthy. Your friend Kaypack succeeded. What is wrong with you, miserable infant? Where is your greatness?"

"I will—I can—I will climb—" But, even as he spoke, the mountain seemed to draw farther away.

"Then do it," cried Sung bitterly.

"I will," said Darcey. He managed no more than a harsh whisper. "I will . . . I will . . ."

"I'm sure you will, dear, but it'll help if you open your eyes first."

Darcey opened his eyes. Maria Novitsky stood grinning above him. "I—I must have been dreaming," Darcey said blankly. About what? He couldn't exactly recall.

"You'll have to put it aside till later. Right now hell's boiling over outside. You and I have to join in."

"It was a dreadful dream," said Darcey.

"Then all the better I came when I did." She boosted him to his feet, where Darcey shook himself. Hurriedly he dressed.

"Why so soon?" he asked, once his thoughts had descended to the present plane. "It wasn't supposed to be today."

"No, but Kaypack's been arrested. Welch said there was nothing he could do."

"In Nova's womb?"

"She wasn't there. Veador was—they hauled him in, too."

"Nova told?"

"She says not."

"Then who?"

Maria shrugged. "I don't think it matters. Maybe Kaypack had a premonition. Last night after the meeting, Kaypack gave Nova the money. She's got it now. It's why we believe it wasn't her."

"I'm ready," Darcey said, moving toward the chute.

"Good. Just don't let anything outside throw you." Maria laughed harshly. "It's crazy out there."

Outside, Darcey understood what she meant. Although only a few people could be seen from here, Darcey could hear what sounded like an enraged mob screaming and shouting from the direction of the central midway. The sky had changed, too, flickering between shades of green and orange, like a broken kaleidoscope. The sight made Darcey feel vaguely ill.

Maria smiled at his discomfort. "I know. Sometimes we expect certain things to be a certain way. When they aren't, it's bad."

"I've never seen a sky like that before."

"Then don't look at it."

Maria headed toward the clamor of the midway. When she reached the mob, she skirted its edge. Darcey, sensing the vastness of the rage surrounding him, said, "I guess Johann did what he was supposed to do."

Maria grinned back. "Him and me both. We didn't see any need to get you till it was time. The casinos lost their pants for three hours straight before shutting down. I've never seen anything that funny in my life."

Darcey noticed a thick cloud of black smoke hanging in the air near the big casino itself, but Maria turned another way. Darcey stepped gingerly past two angry backworlders. One spun on a heel and swung a fist. Darcey ducked and darted by. The fleecie screamed in ranting rage.

"This is awful," said Darcey.

"As it should be," Maria said happily. "Look, these people have to be played like a big orchestra, built up to a final crescendo. We don't want anyone cracking open too soon and blowing the planet apart before we're ready. Welch hasn't even made his announcement yet. I think that's wise. They're ready to blow—close, damn close."

Maria took Darcey through an entrance tube to the top floor of a wide, squat building. "I work here," she explained. "Live here, too."

"Do you need to get something?" They passed a succession of open, gray-walled rooms. In some, young women slept. Maria's room, the last on the corridor, shone as bright as a star in comparison.

"Here," she said, extracting a suit of clothes from the wall. "Put this on."

Darcey peered at the black silken uniform. "Isn't this a security agent's?"

"That's right." She nodded. "It's you, son."

Obediently, Darcey dressed. The suit hung very loosely, especially in the knees and hips, but Maria said, "It'll have to do." She moved toward the corridor. "Hurry."

He followed, panting to keep pace. "Maria, please tell me what this is all about."

"It's Kaypack," she said, over a shoulder. They moved down the long corridor again. "You're the one that's going to set him and Veador free. Here—read this." She removed a folded sheet of paper from some hidden pocket and handed it to Darcey.

He stopped in front of the gaping exit chute and read quickly. The noise of the mob below emerged, though muffled, from the round chute opening. "This is a death warrant." He stared at the paper in horror. "For Commander Kaypack."

She nodded tightly. "I know—I forged it personally."

"It's signed by someone named Blaze."

"He's real enough but that's my writing." She laughed. "Blaze didn't want to take credit."

"Oh." Darcey grinned in relief.

"Come on." Maria dived for the chute. When her feet disappeared from view, Darcey saw no choice but to follow. He rejoined her on the midway, where the crowd swirled like angry insects. Gray and black smoke filled the air. Darcey pressed his hands close to his lips to make breathing easier.

"This way." Maria nudged Darcey toward a nearby building. It was a small black cube, windowless and strangely untouched by the mob. "They're in there," she explained, speaking close to his ear. "Find Welch and show him the warrant. He should turn them over to you."

"And if he can't?"

"Then I guess you'll have to take them out by force."

Darcey was about to ask how that was to be accomplished when Maria gave a final push and propelled him through the narrow entrance chute and into the building itself. Two dozen security agents milled within a single room. Clutching the warrant, Darcey moved through them. At least, he heard Welch's voice reverberating familiarly ahead. "Sir?" cried Darcey, moving swiftly and boldly toward him.

Welch turned and glared without a hint of recognition. "What do you want, boy? There's work to be done outside —not in here." He waved expansively at the crowded room. "I'm saddled with enough cowards as it is."

"An order, sir." Darcey strained to add believability to his voice. "Two prisoners you have."

Welch took the warrent and huffed a bleak sigh. "What will they think of next?" He shook his head. "The poor bastards. At a time like this, too." He passed the paper to the agent standing nearest to him.

"Kaypack and Veador?" said the agent. He glanced quickly at the warrant. "That is too bad."

"Yes," said Welch. One entire wall of the room was occupied by a series of color viewscreens. Each showed a different view of the Paradise Planet midway, and all were presently filled with scenes of raging chaos. Welch retrieved the warrant and called an agent away from the screens. "Take this order into the back and bring me Kaypack and Veador. This young man has a use for them."

The agent walked off with a shrug. A door slid open in the back wall and the agent disappeared through it. When the door closed, Darcey heard the click of an automatic lock.

"They should be out in a moment or two," said Welch, feigning total unconcern.

"Of course," said Darcey, battling to control his nerves. Was it possible? He couldn't help suspecting that they already recognized him as an imposter and were merely biding their minutes before pouncing.

The agent who had been talking with Welch when Darcey

first arrived suddenly reappeared. He scowled at Welch and pointed a finger at Darcey. "Who is this guy, Rickard? I just talked to Blaze at syndicate headquarters and he knows nothing about this."

"That's odd," said Welch, tugging at his lip in apparent puzzlement. "I better look at that warrant."

Just then, the other agent returned through the back wall. Kaypack and Veador moved stiffly in front of him. "Here they are, sir," said the agent.

Welch didn't waste a moment. He grabbed the warrant and appeared to study it closely. "No wonder," he finally said. "Blaze didn't sign this. Calkins did." He handed the warrant back to Darcey, who tried to hide it quickly. Welch waved at the wall of viewscreens. "We better get back to work. Young man"—he meant Darcey—"I hope you won't enjoy your work."

"I don't intend to, sir."

Kaypack, gazing at Darcey, showed no recognition or surprise.

"Let's go," Darcey said, in as gruff a voice as he could manage.

Kaypack hung back. "Are you intending to kill me?"

Welch, who had already turned toward the wall of screens, paused and laid a kind hand on Kaypack's shoulder. "They merely want to ask a few additional questions. I'm sure, if you go along quietly, there'll be no problem."

"Then what's all that?" Kaypack indicated the viewscreens, as Darcey suppressed a groan. Effective acting was fine in its place—but Kaypack was going too far for realism.

"Just a little disturbance," said Welch. "No business of yours. Now—I insist—please get along."

This time Kaypack turned toward the exit chute. Veador shambled in pursuit, and Darcey hurried after him. The hands of both prisoners were bound with plastic shackles, and their pace was necessarily slow. With each step he took, Darcey sensed fastened to his spine the probing eyes of a dozen suspicious agents. The exit chute seemed to stretch endlessly ahead. He was walking forever. Then at last—it happened almost suddenly—he was standing outside on the sawdust of the midway.

He finally dared to turn his head.

No one had followed.

Kaypack, hearing the clamor of the rioters for the first time, said, "My God, what's happening out here? This is a little disturbance?"

"No, sir, this is our plan. Don't you remember?"

"After a night locked up, I hardly remember anything. Here—cut me loose. You'll have to find a sharp knife someplace."

Darcey glanced nervously back at the security building. "Don't you think we should get farther away?"

Kaypack looked angrily at his hands.

"Darcey is correct, my commander," Veador said softly.

"Yes, I suppose he is." Kaypack sighed. "All right, but be damn sure you hurry."

Darcey promised that he would, but still, even when they had passed well out of sight of the building, he preferred to maintain the pretense of being a guard with his prisoners. He didn't feel safe until Maria Novitsky finally emerged from the cover of a small concession and said, "Why don't you let him go?"

"He's afraid I'll try to run for it," said Kaypack angrily.

"No, I'm not," Darcey said. "I need a knife."

"Here—use this." Maria passed him a knife from her belt.

As quickly as his fingers could manage, Darcey cut Kaypack free. "It was close," he told Maria as he worked. "Welch had to help out at the end."

She smiled sardonically. "I'm surprised he was willing to take the risk. While you were inside, the loudspeakers started announcing doom. We're supposed to strike the mother planet in six common hours. Welch must have set a tape, then snuck himself far away."

"Did it fool anyone?" Darcey asked.

"Are you kidding? These fleecies? It fooled every damn one of them. I hope Welch is smart enough to make his run now, because that's exactly what we're going to do. If the time isn't ripe for plucking, then I'm a peach myself."

"But won't the scancircle be impossibly crowded?" asked Kaypack, almost with diffidence. It was plain that his brief imprisonment had somehow lessened his spirit. "If the fleecies believe this planet is about to be destroyed, won't they be fighting to get away?"

"Sure," said Maria, brightly, "and that's why we're going to use a private route. Welch found us an underground passageway that happens to link syndicate headquarters with the scancircle. The others are supposed to meet us there."

"But shouldn't I be set free first, Maria?" said Veador. He held up his hands, still encased in tight plastic strips.

"Oh," said Darcey, moving forward with the knife.

"No," said Maria, grabbing him back. "Veador won't be going with us."

For the first time since his escape, Kaypack showed some feeling. "Maria, you shouldn't give orders to my crew."

"I wasn't giving an order—I was stating a fact. None of us wants to go anywhere with this traitor."

Kaypack looked confused. "A traitor? Veador? You must be mistaken."

"Then who do you think it was who turned you in to security?"

"Well, it certainly wasn't Veador. He and I—"

"Of course it was. And you know damn well it was. Why else did you turn the money over to Nova? You knew what Veador was up to, and you took the precaution."

"I did not. I wanted to be safe. I was cautious—that was all."

"You've never been cautious in your life. So ask him. Get him to deny it."

"What?"

"Ask Veador. I mean it. If he says no, I'll take his word."

But when Kaypack turned to face Veador, there was no need to ask anything. The shame written across Veador's sorrowful face was plain for anyone to read.

"Would you care to explain yourself, Veador?" said Kaypack softly.

"My commander," Veador began. "I carried nothing near to my heart but your own good welfare. Surely you must recognize the madness inherent in this scheme. With the money, we could pay our syndicate debt. We could repair the concession. A new life would open for us—for you."

"A new life here?" said Kaypack in disgust.

"Isn't it better, my commander, than a death out there?" He pointed to the sky—now colored a bright, glowing purple —and shivered.

"No, Veador, it isn't. Not for me. I'm too old. Death no longer holds any dread for me. I would rather die in the midst of life than live in the midst of death."

"That's all very sweet and poetic," Maria interrupted, "but I'm really afraid we have another pressing appointment to keep." The edge of the mob had by now reached even this relatively obscure location. The noise of shouting, screaming, violent men and women nearly drowned out Maria's words. "We have to go now if we don't want to miss the others."

"I'll just be another moment," said Kaypack. Reaching out, he took the knife from Darcey's fingers and began to cut Veador's plastic bindings.

"Are you completely crazy?" Maria cried. "He admitted he was the one."

"He is also my friend."

"A friend who had you locked up in jail."

"Yes, but for his own good, selfless reasons. If we forgave our friends only when they were right, how could we differentiate between them and our enemies?"

Maria shook her head in utter bewilderment and looked at Darcey as if to say, *Are you and I the only sane ones left?*

Darcey, who felt he agreed with Commander Kaypack, could provide no reassurance.

Once Veador was free, with Maria leading, the four of them set off toward the huge bulk of the syndicate headquarters building, where, strangely enough, only a few stray fragments of the mob had gathered. These people—no more than twenty—wandered forlornly through the wide concrete plaza that fronted the big building. Even now there was a mood about the building—something symbolized by its size and blunt angles—that prevented anyone from taking direct action against the rulers who lived inside. Darcey recognized among the fleecies in the plaza Nova, Helsing, and the two Simerians. With a wave, he called them over.

Nova was laughing as she spotted Kaypack. "I knew you could do it," she told Darcey, "and I told Maria so, too. She wanted Helsing to do it, but I said you were the only one of us young enough to pass for a real agent."

Darcey wasn't sure whether he appreciated her assistance, so he simply smiled and let her compliment pass.

"We seem to be missing only Mr. Welch," Helsing observed.

"And he should be along shortly." Maria pointed at the building itself. "Let's creep over this way more. I feel too exposed out here." She coughed. The smoke in the air was growing very thick again.

When Welch arrived shortly after this, he looked worried and out of breath. "They damn near nabbed me," he said. "I was playing with the weather gauges, trying to cook up a windstorm, when my chief assistant bumbled in and demanded to know what I was doing. I had to needle the poor fool." He glared at Darcey. "It was your lousy performance that first aroused his suspicions."

"If you'd been a little more directly helpful," Nova said, "then we wouldn't have had to use Darcey."

"I'm the one who found us this way out, aren't I?" said Welch.

"Both of you shut up," said Maria. "We can fight all we want once we're safe, but let's stow it for now. Welch, since you know where we're going, I suggest you lead."

"All right, fine." He gave Nova a final, lingering glare. "Then let's go." With a certain, purposeful step, Welch headed straight for the building's main entrance. The others followed in a hesitant single file. At the entrance-tube a guard stopped them. Welch uttered a few meaningless phrases, apparently a password, and the guard waved them past. When Darcey went by, followed by the Simerians, the guard blinked furiously but seemed otherwise undisturbed.

Once inside the building—the silence made it seem like a tomb after the constant cacophony outside—Welch turned down a flight of strangely anachronistic manual stairs. Darcey gripped the handrail tightly as he moved down. With each step, he feared that his legs would refuse to support his trailing body.

Nova giggled. "I haven't seen anything like this since I left my home planet."

"It's very old," Welch called back.

"About as old as Kaypack," said Maria.

At the bottom of the stairs was a wide, dim, open room. At one end, a round opening gaped in the high wall. Welch went to it and peered through the hole. "There should be cars here. I can't believe they're all in use."

"I can," Maria said. "I think your syndicate has flown the burning coop."

"We'll have to walk," said Welch.

"How far is it?"

"Perhaps two kilometers."

Maria sniffed the air. Darcey, too, could smell the smoke. "Perhaps we ought to run," she said.

But they walked—quickly. Within the tunnel, a bright yellow light burned, showing a concrete roadway pitted with age. The path refused to progress in a logical, straight line. Instead, the road zigzagged crazily, darting like a snake past unseen obstacles set in the ground above. With each step, Darcey was certain that the odor of smoke grew worse. He began to cough and then could not quit. The tunnel itself disturbed him, with its sleek, cream-colored plastic walls. No one spoke. Nova started coughing, too, and then Helsing as well. The sound of their footsteps boomed like many hollow drums. Darcey perspired thickly. It seemed hot. Reaching out tentatively, he felt the tunnel wall, which was warm to the touch. He drew back his fingers.

Welch announced, "It shouldn't be long now." His voice, amplified by the dead tunnel walls, reverberated lifelessly. "The exit should be right up ahead." The yellow light flickered, then died. As Nova screamed, the light returned. Darcey never lost a step.

After five more minutes—it could have been ten—the tunnel seemed no different, no nearer to ending. Welch broke into a trot. Darcey could hear his gasping breath. The others ran, too, maintaining a steady pace. The Simerians, too fragile for running, soon fell behind. In Darcey, a sense of utter panic grew, spreading like spilled water. They were no longer alone. A deathly, terrible creature—some great silver beast—lurked behind. Darcey fled from its fangs and claws.

By the time the stairs appeared, Darcey ran side by side with Welch. Both men stumbled to a halt and knelt, shoulders touching, upon the first stairstep. Maria arrived next, tumbling between them. Then Helsing, Nova, Veador, and finally Kaypack.

Welch, fully recovered from the ugly fear that had driven him, said, "This opens directly underneath the scancircle. We ought to go now."

Maria began to crawl up the stairs.

Kaypack stopped her with a restraining hand. "No—wait. The Simerians aren't here."

"Damn the Simerians!" cried Welch. "We'll suffocate—we can't wait."

"We will wait," Kaypack said. He positioned himself on

the stairs so that he blocked anyone from passing. "I need a crew."

"A crew of corpses." Welch looked to Nova, who retained the passage money in her purse. "We can knock him aside."

"You can try if you want," said Nova. "But not me."

Welch staggered to his feet.

Just then, the Simerians fell among them. Darcey realized he had been hearing approaching footsteps for some time.

"Let's go," Kaypack said, turning without a backward glance.

Welch pounded up the stairs, but it was Kaypack who led now.

The smoke grew thicker the higher they climbed. Darcey pressed his nose and lips against the thin sleeve of his tunic. Welch opened the heavy iron doors with a key he carried. A burst of red light blinded Darcey. A hot wind, like a physical force, slapped his face. When Darcey could see again, Kaypack had gone through the opening.

The world had been set afire. Smoke rolled across the hard ground in thick, gray waves. It was impossible to see more than a meter directly ahead.

Kaypack shouted, "Get down! We're in the circle! Crouch!"

Darcey, recognizing the concrete at his feet, fell on his face and hugged the ground. He heard Welch scream, "Help me, I'm blind!"

"Quick—give me the money." This was Kaypack's voice —nearby in the gray cloud.

"Here—here it is." Nova.

"Stay where you are! No one move! We'll be gone in a moment!" Kaypack again.

Darcey saw the flickering orange flames rising through the curtain of smoke.

If Kaypack failed to find his way, they all would burn to death.

He heard someone whimpering, but it might have been any one of them. Even, he realized, himself.

Then blackness overwhelmed him and he thought at first that he was dead, but the darkness persisted for the blinking of an eye, and then there was light and someone laughing.

His vision cleared. He lay sprawled on his side, supported by a hard, cold steel floor.

It was Kaypack who was laughing. "Damn them all!" he was shouting. "Damn their poor demented souls! We made it! I'm back! Do you hear me? I'm back where I belong!"

It was then that Darcey understood that the crew of the *Arjuna* had reached its new home at last.

"It seemed unnecessarily long and detailed," said a child.

"What?" I couldn't prevent showing my surprise. "But it was supposed to be exciting."

"I think you're underestimating us again. We knew they'd escape all along. The story's about the grayspace beast, right?"

"Well, largely, yes," I admitted.

"So how could there be a grayspace beast, while everyone's stuck on Paradise Planet? With that in mind, the episode carries about as much real suspense as watching you get up in the morning."

"I don't think you know much about classical drama. For instance, the mood of a story is properly generated by—"

"He must be Darcey," said a girl.

This surprised me so much—coming when it did—that I impulsively violated my best intentions and asked, "What makes you think that?"

She laughed (at me). "Because only Darcey—shut up all his life—could try to feed us those hoary old precepts and expect to get away with it."

I was hurt. Not a young being, I was sensitive about my age. "All right," I said, drawing myself up into a rather silly pout, "if that's the way you want it, that's the way you'll get it. From now on, the story's going to be about as exciting and action-filled as one of your class seminars."

They all laughed at that, too—properly so, I later realized. With a story like mine, the imposition of dullness was quite impossible.

I still knew I was going to blow their heads off later on.

THREE

"Now about this beast again," said one.

I smiled. "It's coming."

"In the flesh?" She seemed doubtful.

"In what passes for beast flesh."

"Now?"

"Oh, no." I saw the need to backtrack quickly. "We just got our crew aboard the ship. I've got to set the scene, twirl the characters, uncover their conflicting motivations. I can't just throw the beast at you right away."

"Why not?" She gave me her high-energy glare.

"That wouldn't be very believable, would it? You don't want me to sacrifice suspense in return for a cheap thrill."

"Sure I do."

"Well, you're not going to get it this time. I've got a ship and crew to describe."

Kaypack established the following general schedule for his crew: sixteen hours of intensive specific training in each crew position; eight hours in which to eat, sleep, hobnob, rest, and relax; sixteen further hours of intensive specific training.

Darcey couldn't speak for the others, but the best he personally could manage with his eight free hours was a tepid meal from the fortunately large store of ship's provisions and then a dull, deep, never-restful sleep in the crowded womb of the lower crew quarters. Darcey knew he had never worked this hard in his entire life, and he suspected that the others felt the same, for their murmured complaints provided a standard background to any moment he shared with them.

Yet even they had to admit that no matter how hard they worked, Kaypack worked even harder. Not only did he teach the other eight their varied duties, but once the day's training period was completed, he retired to his own stateroom, where he sat up most of the eight-hour break, preparing the next day's lessons. If Kaypack ever found time to eat a cooked meal, no one ever caught him at it. He seemed capable of functioning on a diet of reserve energy alone.

Because of the limited amount of food on board the cruiser and the impossibility of bringing additional supplies from Paradise Planet, the sooner they commenced their first exploratory journey, the better. Kaypack set their anticipated flight date two common months subsequent to their arrival at the ship. In spite of the immense quantity of work to be completed first, Kaypack continued to insist that this date be met.

Each of the eight had been assigned a crew position immediately upon arrival. Darcey's assignment as assistant ship's navigator had not originally pleased him. Johann Helsing knew so much about complex mathematics and computer technology that there seemed little for Darcey himself to do. Soon enough, however, he learned of Kaypack's strong belief that any decent assistant must know as much (preferably more) than his supposed superior. For Darcey, whose mathematical knowledge barely extended to the concept of infinity, this meant a formidable amount of learning in a very short time. It further meant, during those infrequent moments when Kaypack himself was not assigning some particularly sticky problem in grayspace navigation, that Helsing was showing Darcey how to determine the square root of an imaginary number or the method for computing the area of a trapezoid when the lengths of two unequal sides were known. During rest periods, the moment he shut his eyes, a terrible stream of numbers, letters, figures, and symbols rushed across the backsides of Darcey's eyes. It was no wonder, when

Kaypack's shrill whistle blew and Darcey awoke, that he seldom felt as if he had slept at all.

Veador was appointed crew chief and engineer and given two assistants to help him in the engine room: the Simerians. Needless to say, Veador complained bitterly about this, but Kaypack pointed out that the Simerians might well be more experienced than Veador at running fusion engines and that to assign them elsewhere would only needlessly cripple the crew. Kaypack did offer to let Veador resign his position so that the Simerians could be appointed in his place, but Veador quickly managed to swallow his prejudice and agreed to serve his commander obediently. Once, when passing through the engine room, Darcey caught sight of the three of them—Veador and his Simerian associates—bent over with their heads thrust inside the gaping cavity of the central grayspace drive. The sight of these three strange behinds, two slim and pale, the third green with a stiff tail, caused Darcey to break into a burst of uncontrollable laughter. Swinging a heavy wrench, Veador whirled and chased Darcey the length of the corridor.

Rickard Welch agreed to serve as executive officer and assistant pilot, but because Kaypack quickly assumed the actual functions of both these positions, Welch was assigned further duty as assistant alien specialist, serving under Maria Novitsky. Theoretically at least, the alien specialists bore the most complicated duties aboard the ship, for their work demanded the broadest knowledge. Whenever the ship actually reached an alien world, it was the responsibility of the specialists to first determine if the planet was even worth investigating. If they said yes, then their work immediately extended into such fields as geology, botany, meteorology, and, if intelligent life was found, alien psychology. In spite of the complexity of these duties, Kaypack actually spent very little time working with Maria or Welch. As a result, the two of them were often together in the crew quarters, dreaming of future riches and complaining of current sufferings. Darcey thought he knew the reason behind Kaypack's lack of interest in training the alien specialists, but it was not something he would ever dare reveal. (It was the beast, of course.)

Nova, finally, was allowed to be the cruiser serf—she scrubbed the ship and cooked the meals. The former task she did well enough, but the latter required a great deal of intensive training. Welch, for one, complained that he was forced to go around with a permanent bellyache.

Nor was Nova especially pleased with the duties assigned her. In fact, she spent many hours huddled beside Darcey—who was trying to study—in the control room. She often spoke of Commander Kaypack. "He's senile," she said.

Darcey looked up from the navigation charts in front of him. "Oh, I don't think—"

"Then he's just mean, cruel, vicious. He's trying to pay me back for what I did to him on Paradise Planet."

"But he was the one who insisted on having you aboard."

"So what? He couldn't pay me back if I wasn't here."

"But Veador acted much worse than you. He isn't trying to pay Veador back."

"Are you sure about that?" She laughed bitterly. "Why do you think those Simerians are down in the engine room? Kaypack knows damn well Veador can't stand the sight of them."

"Oh, that doesn't make sense. Commander Kaypack isn't petty."

"No, but he's sly—and mean."

"He is not. He assigned everyone the jobs they could do best. Here, you tell me, Nova." He always said this when his patience wore thin. "Name one job on this ship you could perform better than the person who's doing it now."

She grinned. "That's easy."

He folded his arms. "Then name it."

"All right: yours. You can barely add two and two."

He pouted. "Well, I'm trying to learn."

"I could learn a lot faster," she said mockingly.

"Oh, let me alone."

But she never did.

All of this time, one question remained uppermost in Darcey's mind: When would Kaypack get around to revealing the real nature of their mission? So far, except for himself, the crew remained ignorant of the beast. He knew that Kaypack would have to handle this point with the utmost tact. Welch and Maria, most obviously, would object. Nor could Helsing or Nova be expected to be pleased. Veador knew of the beast but feared it.

Darcey both wished that the question would be settled and worried that when it was there would be even more trouble as a result.

On each seventh day, during the final hour of training time, Kaypack gathered the crew in the barren cavern of the ship's lounge to deliver what he termed a history lesson. Apparently, it was Kaypack's opinion that no one could truly serve as a stellar until he was made aware of the tremendous heritage built up by those who had preceded him into space. Darcey found each lesson quite enthralling. He learned of man's earliest ventures to the moons and planets of his own system, the invention of the grayspace drive, the creation of the stellar service, and the glorious era of interstellar exploration. Welch and Maria said the lectures were boring. Nova said she didn't care; anything was better than cooking or cleaning. Twice she fell soundly asleep while Kaypack discussed the wondrous years when both he and the galaxy were young.

Darcey could not think of any worse place or time to reveal the secret of the beast.

It happened during the fourth weekly lesson.

Kaypack began calmly enough, with no hint of what was to follow. "Today I want to talk to you of certain peripheral matters related to space travel. The legends, myths, and fables that have grown up around—"

"Are you speaking of yourself?" said Welch with a wide grin. He sat upon a wide couch, Maria at his feet.

Whether this remark stung Kaypack and drove him to what followed, Darcey was never able to decide.

Kaypack glared at Welch. "I was thinking more in terms of the grayspace beast."

Only Darcey showed any emotion at this announcement. He let his jaw drop in surprise and tried to interrupt: "But, sir, shouldn't we—?"

Welch spoke louder. "Not that hoary old tale. Damn it, Kaypack, why won't you let us go to bed?"

"I consider this to be important." Kaypack spoke with such feeling that Welch became instantly suspicious.

"Why? Have you seen this famous beast?"

No, no, thought Darcey. *Don't answer. Tell him to go to hell. Don't—please don't.*

But Kaypack, driven by impulses beyond logic, went heedlessly on. "The reality of the beast can hardly be doubted."

"Then you have met this creature?" Welch prodded, his eyes maliciously glowing. "You've come eyeball to eyeball?"

"I have," said Kaypack.

"Then tell us about it."

"Sure," Maria said. "Give us the thrill of a lifetime."

Darcey glanced around the wide room. He observed the anxiety on Veador's face, the curiosity on Nova's, and the confusion on Helsing's. Only the Simerians seemed totally unmoved. They huddled in a single chair, bodies pressed snugly together, oblivious to everything outside themselves.

Kaypack was speaking. "The grayspace beast is a creature formed from pure energy. It's bigger than this cruiser and lurks in the vacuum we call grayspace. When a human ship dares to invade its lair, the beast springs forth. It may kill. It may maim. More often, it will drive men mad."

There was a singsong, lilting tone to Kaypack's voice that caused Darcey to shiver. He tried to catch Veador's eye.

They must get the commander out of here. In a few more moments it would be too late.

But Welch was enjoying himself too tremendously to stop now. The tedium of the training period made itself known in his refusal to quit. "Is that what happened to you, commander? This beast sprang forth and shoved you over the brink?"

Maria laughed aloud.

Kaypack looked sad. "My own confrontations with the beast were fortunately without harm—to either of us. But I've seen other men—good men, strong men. I've seen the terrible madness burning in their eyes. Veador here can confirm the truth of that."

Veador who everyone present knew had never entered grayspace in his life, said bleakly, "My commander speaks only the truth."

Helsing and Nova joined the laughter this time.

"Oh, shut up," Darcey told Nova, who sat closest to him.

"Why? He's funny."

"He can't help himself."

"So? Neither can I."

Darcey sprang to his feet. As soon as he opened his mouth, he knew this was a mistake, but it was too late to stop now. "He's telling the truth. There is a beast. My parents saw it. They told me about it, too."

He only hoped that would be sufficient to satisfy them and that the subject of the beast could be discarded until a later, better moment. But Welch laughed derisively and turned to face Darcey. "Naturally, they'd tell you that. Why not? It's a marvelously creepy story, delightful for children. But, good God, man—" he now faced Kaypack again, "I expected better of you. By definition, grayspace is simply empty space—nothing can be alive there."

"The true purpose of this mission . . ." said Kaypack, oblivious to all else. He stood as if in a trance, his eyes wide open, his body still. "We must find and slay the grayspace beast. Until now I have kept this secret from you, but now, with our training nearing completion, I feel it is time you knew the truth. Shortly we will enter the wastes of grayspace. There, we will seek out this monstrous beast and destroy it. Our task is a bold—"

Welch glowered with rage. "Wait a damn minute. What are you trying to say? The purpose of this mission is to exploit what hasn't been exploited. We're going to get rich—not chase some fantasy beast."

"I think the beast wants to gobble Kaypack up," said Maria.

Kaypack continued talking. His voice dropped to a dull monotone and only infrequent words—"beast," "monster," "kill," "grayspace"—could be heard.

"Wait," Darcey pleaded, with tears in his eyes. "Listen to him—please—this is important. He's not crazy."

"If he's not," Nova said, "he's sure putting on a marvelous imitation."

Welch came over and stood beside Darcey. "Do you mean to say he's serious, boy?"

"Yes," said Darcey bleakly. "It's the Radians, you see, the people on the planet where I was born. When they sent me to Commander Kaypack, with the ship and the money, they said it was to kill the beast."

"Then they're crazy, too," said Welch.

"No, they aren't. Don't you people have any imagination—don't you care about anything?" Past Welch, Darcey saw Veador leading Kaypack from the room. The sight strangely enraged him, and he went on with even more feeling than before. "There is a beast. Commander Kaypack knows that. The elders—the Radians—wouldn't lie about that. All any of you care about is money. Until a month ago, I never even knew there was such a thing and it didn't hurt me any. Commander Kaypack is a great man, and you think that means he's stupid. Well, I think you're the stupid ones. You, Mr.

Welch, and you, Maria, and Johann, and Nova, too. You're so stupid you think the truth is funny."

Welch snorted, Maria laughed, Helsing stared at the floor, embarrassed, and Nova started to argue. The Simerians, as always, remained locked inside their private cosmos.

Ignoring them, Darcey turned on a heel and left the lounge. He hurried to catch up with Veador and Kaypack, but he was already too late for that.

"Oh-oh, you blew it again," said one of the older boys.

"Now what?" I suppose my patience was beginning to wear thin. "Don't you like what Darcey said?"

"It's not Darcey I'm worried about, it's Kaypack. Where's the motivation for his crazy outbrust? One second, he's fine, teaching everyone how to run the ship, and the next he's raving like a maniac."

"Now you sound like Welch. Nothing Kaypack said was untrue."

"No, but you've got to admit that the way he said it—or the way you had him say it—was a bit excessive."

"Not if you understand the motivation," I said smugly.

That got them mad, all right. "That's just what I said." They all started hollering then.

I decided to take pity and explain. "He's scared—can't you understand that—Kaypack is scared to death of the beast. He did lie to them—I thought you'd see that. Kaypack's never seen the beast. If he had he'd know what he was into, but he hasn't and he doesn't."

"He said all of that crazy stuff because he was afraid?"

"Sure, wouldn't you? Think about it for a moment. Kaypack wants to get back into space. It's his whole life and without it he's dead. The opportunity comes along and he jumps at it. The trouble is, the opportunity demands he risk his own life in payment. He doesn't want to do that. He just wants to see the stars, travel the spacelanes. He doesn't want to die. For a month, he worries about it. How can he manage to extract himself from this mess? Finally, the answer hits him. Without a crew behind him he can hardly go beast hunting. So, deliberately, he breaks the news to the crew in the worst possible way imaginable. They turn on him —they say no—he's done his best and been beat. I told you when I started this story that Kaypack was a sly, calculating man. Maybe next time, when I tell you something, you'll bother to listen."

"Maybe you did tell us," said the same boy again, "but that's just words. There's nothing like that in the story itself."

"Sure, there is. I thought you wanted me to be subtle. It's there—it's implicit."

While they were busily engaged struggling to answer that, I hastily went on with the story. *Hoo-hah*. Slipped free again.

The door to Kaypack's stateroom hung open—all doors aboard the *Arjuna* were old manual contraptions—and Darcey peeped through. He saw Kaypack sprawled upon the tattered mattress of an unkempt bunk, and the stillness and silence of the room drew him farther.

Veador sat beside the bunk and, seeing Darcey looked up sadly. "He does not feel well."

Darcey saw what Veador meant. Although he lay as rigid as a corpse, Kaypack held his eyes wide open and stared at the ceiling above.

"Those bastards," said Darcey, his anger rising again. "That Welch."

Veador moved slightly. He shrugged. "What did he or the others say that was not true? For long this beast has obsessed my poor commander. When it enters his mind, he thinks of nothing else."

Darcey could not budge his eyes from Kaypack's stiff, staring form. "You shouldn't say that, Veador."

"I merely try to serve my commander."

"Then serve him properly. There is a beast. He spoke the truth."

Veador remained unconvinced. He stood up slowly and edged toward the door. "Perhaps I should consult with the others."

"If you wish," said Darcey.

"There is no work for me here. I have known the commander too long. When he reaches this state, he exists in another world."

"I'll stay with him."

"I will return."

"Don't hurry yourself."

Alone with Kaypack, Darcey dropped into the place Veador had vacated. The instant he did, a sudden change fell across Kaypack's features. His muscles relaxed and his eyes blinked. Slowly he swiveled his head and looked at Darcey. "Is that you?" he asked in a dull, hollow voice.

"It's Darcey, sir."

"Oh, yes—you." Kaypack turned his eyes to the ceiling again. "I was afraid you'd come. I botched it, didn't I?"

"No, sir."

"You're too kind, Darcey. You know what my mistake was? I overestimated them. The training had gone so well I began to think of them as genuine stellars. Why not tell them the truth? I wondered. They're good people—they can take it. I was wrong. Even Veador. I heard him just now. For two hundred years, I thought he believed in me."

"Don't listen to what Veador says, sir. You know he loves you."

"Does he?" Kaypack chuckled. "Perhaps so—but why? Because of me? Or because of his alien laws? Once, long ago, Veador agreed to serve me. I thought it was for a few days; he thought it was for a lifetime. We both made silly mistakes. About fifty years ago—this is a confession—I got tired of him. There was a young woman—never mind who, because she's not young anymore—and we fell in love for an instant or two. She didn't like Veador, or he, her. She wanted to go away. We went together. Another planet. A beautiful place.

Trees, flowers, streams—everything Paradise Planet lacks. We got mad at each other—we fought. How come? Boredom, I guess. Eventually we both came back. I found Veador. In all the time I was gone, he hadn't eaten a bite. He hadn't slept. He was dying. Why? I asked him as soon as he recovered. Did I mean that much to him? He told me coldly: no. It was the ironclad law of his people. He had agreed to serve me. If he failed, he was dead. When he spoke, I saw in his eyes something I hadn't noticed before. Veador wanted me to die. Until I did, he wasn't free. I could kill him—I nearly had—but there was nothing he could do to me."

"Sir, that's not true."

Kaypack looked at Darcey with an expression as intense as the core of a star. "Darcey, is there such a creature as the grayspace beast?"

"Yes, sir, I believe there is."

"But you don't know?"

"How could I?"

"Would it interest you if I admitted that I don't know, either? Darcey, I've never seen that beast."

"I know that, sir."

Kaypack sat up, surprised but intrigued. "You know that but you don't know about the beast?"

"It's different with the elders. I can tell when people are lying or not—but not the elders."

Kaypack looked like a beaten man. He dropped back on the bunk and held his head. "Then tell me what we're going to do now, Darcey."

"I think there's only one thing we can do, sir, and that's go on. I think you should rest until the next training period and then just start as if nothing had happened at all."

"They won't forget."

"I don't want them to. Let them know about the beast. But there's only one way we can prove it to them for sure."

"How's that?"

"Show it to them."

Kaypack nodded slowly. "That's true."

"And we're going into grayspace one way or the other no matter what. Isn't that right? If the beast's there, we'll find it."

"I never saw it. Not in two hundred years."

"But we're the first ones. In centuries. Don't you think it'll come to see?"

Kaypack seemed to be thinking of something else—something that existed beyond the boundaries of Darcey's words. "You're right," he said. "I can't have grayspace without the grayspace beast."

"Nor can they."

"Do they want it?"

"They want the money."

Kaypack extended a frail hand. Darcey clasped it. "Then we're going," said Kaypack.

Smiling, Darcey said, "Yes, sir, we are."

"I'll do it just the way you said—I'll wait."

"I think that's best, sir."

"Darcey," said Kaypack, with feeling, "so do I."

Gliding in slow rotation, the grayspace cruiser *Arjuna* swung a wide orbit around the dull orb of the obscure red-giant sun around which the Radian elders had long ago placed the craft. If the red star had once possessed native planets of its own, these worlds had centuries past been consumed within its hot, expanding circumference. The possibility intrigued Darcey. What mighty races or vast civilizations might once have resided here? Where were they now? Snuffed out—extinguished—and why? For no good reason other than the fact that they (mighty race, vast civilization) had failed to possess the necessary outward urge to carry them beyond the ticking time bomb of their own glowing sun. Had the elders deliberately chosen this location as a sign? Be humble, ye people of the Earth. A gentle tickle on the skin of fate and this could be your destiny, too.

In due time, Earth's sun would follow this same cosmic pattern, and the ancient homeworld of mankind would become a cinder of dead ash. What would happen then? Would those billions of human beings scattered across the winking expanse of the galaxy pay more than a brief, backward, nostalgic glance at where they had all originated? Men were not unique, not exceptional—too many other intelligent species had been found—but they were different. It was that relentless, restless outward urge. Why? Darcey, whose knowledge of human ways was limited, could not attempt to answer this question, but Commander Kaypack said that many scholars now believed the answer was a matter of evolutionary history. Humanity had commenced existence as a race of omnivorous scavengers; survival itself demanded constant movement. The wider a man ranged, the greater his chances to live. The pattern was not easily broken. After thousands of generations, the galaxy itself was spanned. But some decline had surely set in; the outward urge had lessened of late. Some mutation in the human psyche had occurred that allowed men to sit and wait at their own ease; the scancircle replaced the grayspace cruiser. Kaypack admitted that he, himself, was a simple throwback. He moved outward because he could not rest. When the Earth died, few men would perish with it. No mighty race—no vast civilization. Kaypack (and those other stellars like him) had saved the human race from certain, cosmic death. Who thanked him? Where was their gratitude? Now Kaypack himself was approaching a weary end. The outward urge remained, a vestigial organ. When Kaypack was gone, none could step forward to assume his role.

At the conclusion of two months' severe training, Commander Kaypack, piloting the interplanetary fusion drive, broke the *Arjuna* free from orbit. Turning majestically upon its axis, the ship drove outward. Kaypack manned the central controls. Veador, with the assistance of the two Simerians, managed the creaking engine. Helsing prepared the grayspace navigation chart to be used in computing a proper jumping place. Nova, Darcey, Maria, and Welch watched the four large viewscreens that composed the walls of the control room. The big red sun gave a distinct jerk. There was no accompanying feeling of acceleration or motion. Spinning in his chair, Kaypack announced, "We are now moving into outer space at a rate of thirty-five thousand kilometers per hour." Darcey again stared at the viewscreens, but nothing had changed.

"Oh, you won't see it there for some time," Kaypack said. "On the cosmic scale, we're still creeping like a worm. I want to exercise the engine before letting it run."

"Then what do we do now?" asked Welch.

"I'll assign watches later." Kaypack glowed with pride—or satisfaction. "Right now let's just enjoy ourselves."

"How?" asked Welch.

For the first time in nearly three centruies, a grayspace ship sent ripples of motion flowing through the galaxy.

Yet—except for the nine crew members aboard, six of whom were human and three were not—no one took the slightest note of the event.

On a cosmic scale, the event was of no greater consequence than the extinction of a minor sun.

In the crew quarters below, Rickard Welch shook Maria Novitsky gently awake and, when she opened her eyes at last, placed a finger across her lips and said, "Hush." The two of them were alone in the tiny cramped room. "I want to talk to you."

"Sure." Maria rubbed the sleep from her eyes. "What about?"

Welch spoke nervously, straining to keep his voice from rising to a frantic pitch. "I was just about to go into the control room a few minutes ago when I stopped. Darcey and Nova are on duty. I overheard them talking about that beast thing."

"So?" Maria sat on the edge of her bunk. "Kids like to talk about that sort of thing."

"But the boy, Darcey, still keeps talking as if those aliens of his really did send him here to get Kaypack to kill this beast."

Space travel did not seem to agree with Welch. He had been acting strangely, like a suddenly caged animal, ever since the *Arjuna* broke free of orbit. Maria tried to be mollifying. "So what? A mythical beast is a mythical beast. It doesn't matter how many aliens believe in it. If it doesn't exist, then it just doesn't."

"But what if it does?" Welch said heatedly. "Then all our plans are ruined."

"No, listen," Maria said. "Let me tell you a story about a planet, Zastro, where I was born. It was ninety per cent ocean, and the colonial population—maybe ten thousand of us—inhabited scattered islands. There were natives, too—barely intelligent—fish who flew—and their chief legend concerned vast sea monsters. Unfortunately, like any good story, it made sense. With those huge oceans, how could anybody believe they didn't contain monsters a hundred meters long with flashing teeth the size of a grown man? I knew brave men who wouldn't go out of sight of shore from pure fear of being eaten alive by monsters. Had anybody seen these creatures? Nope—not me, not anybody I knew, not anybody they knew—but they all thought they had. It was always a fleeting glimpse. An ominous shape in the fog. If a fishing boat strayed too far from shore and never returned, what happened? Sea monster—what else? Never a storm, a log, a leak, always a monster. When I got big and got my own boat, I said the hell with that. If I haven't seen it, then it doesn't exist, and I went out farther than anyone ever had and laid my nets. In a common-year's time, I was rich by local standards. I was also alive, unhurt, and un-sea-monstered. Did my example work? Was there a stampede of boats to follow in my wake? You bet there wasn't. The rest of them just stood around, glaring at my profits and waiting for the day when I got gobbled up. It never came. I scanned away from Zastro and found new and easier ways of living."

Welch nodded thoughtfully. "I see your point."

"I thought you would."

"Then you're convinced the beast doesn't exist?"

She nodded. "At least until I see it."

"And if you do?"

"Then I'll head back to Zastro and take another look at those sea monsters, too."

In the engine room, Johann Helsing squinted to see past Veador's green, glistening shoulders and into the churning innards of the big interplanetary fusion drive. In theory at least, Helsing understood more clearly than anyone else aboard why this engine functioned as it did, but when it came time to putting theory to practical use, his mind somehow balked at the prospect and skidded to a surprising halt.

Helsing backed away, gazing hopelessly at the Simerians cuddled nearby. "I'm afraid I'm just not following you, Veador, but thanks."

"It really is not terribly complex," said Veador. He closed the engine from view. "I could repeat my explanation, if you so desire."

"No, that won't be necessary." Helsing hated to be patronized by this alien. "I was merely curious, thought I'd see what a real engine looked like."

"I could show you the grayspace drive," Veador said.

Helsing started. "It's not functioning, is it?"

"No, of course not, but I could show it to you. My commander says we must be prepared to jump at any moment."

"We won't reach the jumping point for another three days," Helsing said.

"My commander says such figures are never exact."

"Mine are." It pleased Helsing to be able to patronize the alien in turn. "Exactly correct."

Veador sat down on a wooden bench across the room from

the Simerians. He curled his tail beneath him and continued to display an uncommon eagerness to talk. "Entering grayspace will be a unique experience for all of us. Excluding my commander, of course."

"I only know the mathematics of it." Helsing was ready to leave. He glanced furtively at the door. Nothing more than a whim, perhaps a pang of loneliness, had brought him here. Why did the alien insist on chattering?

"And there is this other thing as well," Veador said casually. "This grayspace beast."

"Oh, yes, that." Helsing wasn't surprised. The closer the ship came to its jumping point, the more frequently conversation turned to the beast. "You're not afraid, are you?"

"No, of course not. Why should I be?" Veador paused, shaking his own hands. "And yet one cannot help wondering? Does this creature actually exist?"

"Why ask me?" Helsing felt strangely angered. It was the Simerians, he realized at last. They were watching him. "I don't know any more about it than you do."

"But you must have an opinion."

"I suppose I do." Removing his spectacles from the bridge of his nose, Helsing cleaned the lenses with his open shirt. "No, I don't believe such a creature exists. Theoretically, it's quite impossible. Grayspace is empty space, a true and total vacuum. Nothing can live there."

"Then I must tell you something that has recently risen to disturb me." Veador leaned forward, elbows upon his knees. Plainly, he appeared ready to talk for some time. "On my home planet, Maya—only recently have I recalled this—I am a young creature. Among my relations are five males who have served in the stellar service. Two spoke to me of this beast."

"They claimed to have seen it?" Helsing said.

"Both, yes, and one told me he was actually swallowed by the beast. I recalled this narrative only recently and have mentioned it to no one else. My relative served as the crew chief aboard a cruiser occupied by nine human stellars. The beast appeared in grayspace and chased the ship. The commander, a very brave man, showed true fear for the first time in his life. The beast surrounded the ship, swallowed it, held it within the grasp of its body. My relative spoke of a third universe, one neither grayspace nor normal space. Living creatures dwelled within the beast, entities neither human nor Mayan but alive. The crew of the ship went quickly mad. My relative, for his own safety, was forced to kill each of them in turn. In the end, through a force of will unique to our race, he grasped the ship's controls and jumped blindly into normal space. For ten common years he drifted, lost and alone, darting in and out of grayspace. The beast did not reappear. If it had, his resistance weakened, he would have taken his own life. Eventually, in a freak of good fate, he chanced upon a world inhabited by humans. He told a tale filled with lies. A court of inquiry, though suspicious, cleared him of legal blame. Nonetheless, his commander dead, my relative resigned from the stellar service and retired to peaceful Maya. I recall him clearly. The young seldom approached his abode. He was an odd creature. He frightened us in shameful, painful ways."

"But why tell me all this?" Helsing's anger propelled him toward the door. "It's none of my business—it isn't."

The Simerians stared curiously after him.

Alone among the debris of his stateroom, Kail Kaypack attempted to decide once and for all if he was really the man for this job.

Certain facts stood out. Although he had saddled himself with a crew of amateurs, now, after two months' training, they were exceptionally gifted amateurs. The ship itself, in spite of its age and ill use, was a more than adequate vehicle. The engines were in superb condition. He had little fear from mechancial failure.

No, it was simply the beast alone that made everything else

so much more difficult. It lurked throughout the inner corridors. It mocked him. *Here I am*, it called. *If you can, catch me. Kill me. I'm stronger than you, and wiser. I can kill you.*

His crew did not believe—the vast majority of them, at least. A month ago in the lounge—halfheartedly, he admitted —he had attempted to convince them and failed miserably. Of them all, he suspected that only Darcey and the Simerians truly believed in the physical existence of the grayspace beast.

And the fact was that he himself did not believe. He couldn't.

Centuries past on Earth during the first great human religious age, most sects had believed mankind to be the direct personal creation of divine hands.

Later, as men slowly increased their knowledge of the outer universe, this belief eroded. With the discovery of other intelligent races, it was finally rendered absurd.

The more men learned of what lay outside themselves, the more they reduced their own conception of themselves, and in doing that they further rejected any belief in the divine.

In order to accept the beast as real, that belief was necessary. Darcey held it. The Simerians did. The beast violated everything men had seen and learned during their long outward quest in search of apparent wisdom.

The beast was an unreasonable thing. Therefore, it could not exist.

But if it did?

Kaypack shook his head. It was this one question that prevented him from sleeping at night.

Because (and he admitted this) even if he did not believe in the beast, neither did he yet disbelieve.

I had been expecting one or another of the students to interrupt me for some time, so, when they finally did, their voices came at me like a raging storm. "Wait, wait," I called, raising my voice to a shout. "One at a time, please." I pointed to a blond girl curled in the first row. "You first."

"I want to know about Kaypack," she said. "Are you making him up, or did people really feel that way back then?"

"They did," I said. "They had no reason not to. Nothing they had seen had ever contradicted those beliefs, and they only accepted what they saw."

"That's stupid."

"We think so now." I pointed to another raised hand. "Yes?"

"I want to know what you're trying to prove with all this reverie. You're not just killing time, I assume, filling up space. What's the point?"

I thought that was a fair question, worthy of an answer: "I'm trying to show several things at once. First, these people whom you knew on Paradise Planet, they've all changed significantly since the last time we took a close look at them. Space does that to people. So does grayspace. You'll see that, too, shortly. Secondly, I wanted to indicate that the beast remained very much on everyone's mind. After the incident in the lounge, Darcey wanted to banish it by ignoring it and that didn't work. It didn't even work for himself. Thirdly, because of some past confusion and even argument, I wanted to give a clearer picture of what was happening in Kaypack's mind. We decided he was afraid of the beast. I wanted to show you why. And, fourthly, I wanted the chance to tell some good stories."

"And the Simerians? Is that number five?"

The comment caught me by surprise. "Huh?"

"Well," said the boy, "I couldn't help noticing. You've shown us Darcey, Kaypack, Nova, Veador, Welch, Maria, even Helsing, at close hand. That leaves only the Simerians. We don't even know their names. This time you kept hinting about them. They stared at Helsing and bugged him. Kaypack says they believe in the beast. I think you're building up to something. What?"

"I can hardly tell you that now."

"But there is something?"

I pretended not to have heard. "Any more questions?"

"Yeah," said a girl, fixing me with a stare. I knew something was coming. "Which one of the Simerians is you?"

"The one on the left," I said, and went on with my story.

If any moment in Darcey's life could match the disappointment he'd felt upon meeting his first other men, then that moment would have to be now.

Grayspace!

The word itself pulsed with evocation. A mysterious realm. The second universe. A cosmic place.

Instead, the one awe-inspiring aspect of grayspace was its total emptiness. After that, as the name hinted, it was gray. As the name further implied, it was also space. And that was it. Grayspace was empty gray space, and after ten minutes of gaping and staring, Darcey decided it was nothing more than a vast, cosmic bore.

He stood watch with the Simerians in the control room. The four screens showed the same bleak view of gray waste. Darcey preferred to look at the floor. Tilting his chair, he stared at the high ceiling. He studied his own hands and peered at his booted feet. Anything, he decided, was more interesting than all that emptiness. He let the Simerians handle the duty of watching for the beast.

Actually, during his very first watch, when he'd still been willing to stare at the screens, he'd spotted the beast.

It had happened this way: Within the first hour (of a scheduled twelve-hour watch) Darcey discovered that his eyes were stinging and his head was throbbing with a tension ache. After the second hour, he felt physically ill and found that he could not prevent his mouth from continuing a regular series of wide yawns. In the third hour, he glimpsed the beast. It appeared in the middle of the right viewscreen. It was round, silver, and relatively huge.

Springing to his feet with a delighted yip, Darcey spun to tell the Simerians of his discovery. In doing so, he blinked, and the beast immediately disappeared from the screen.

Darcey sat down. He stared for a long moment and the beast reappeared. He turned, blinked, and the beast vanished.

Finally, he asked the nearest Simerian, who seemed to be watching the same screen, "Did you notice anything just then? A movement—a thing?"

"Such as the grayspace beast?" The Simerians, as always, spoke in unison.

Darcey aimed his voice between them. "Well, yes, something like that."

"No," they said.

"What about right now?" He stood up, eyes unblinking, and crossed to the screen. Touching the place where the beast lurked, he felt a tingle of terror ripple his spine. "Right there."

"Nothing."

Darcey blinked. "Yes, I suppose you're right."

After that, he tried to avoid staring at the screens too long. Later he learned that Nova and Maria had also spotted the beast during their initial watches. Both soon learned to blink. They didn't stare at the screens anymore, either.

The trip through grayspace was scheduled to take eighteen common days. Kaypack had chosen their destination—a G-type star never visited by human crews before. Helsing showed Darcey the place on one of his charts, but it was just another yellow dot, nothing special at all.

Three watches had been established—the twenty-four-hour common day meant nothing in this emptiness: Darcey and the Simerians; Nova and Helsing; Welch and Maria. Veador remained in the engine room—he even slept there now—and Kaypack alternated between his own stateroom and the control room.

The biggest problem Darcey faced was simple boredom. He tried to sleep during Nova's watches, and thus spent the other twelve hours following her around the ship as she performed her serf duties. She complained often. She had already scrubbed the ship from bow to stern—which wasn't true—and then back again. Kaypack hated her. Kaypack tortured her. Once Darcey told her about the time on his first watch when he had thought he'd seen the beast.

Nova turned away from the wall she was scrubbing and laughed. "Well, I hope you manage to spot it again."

"Really?" He knew she didn't believe in the reality of the beast. "Why?"

"Because I want it to come creeping up here and swallow us up, that's why. Look at this." She showed Darcey her hands, which looked quite normal to him. "See what they are? Red. Blood-raw red. Who does that clown think he is? Commander Kail Kaypack. On Paradise Planet, he was a crank in a clown's suit and silly hat. Out here, he's suddenly the syndicate boss of the whole universe. I just wish that beast of his would sneak in here and gobble him up sometime when he's asleep. If he ever does sleep, that is."

Darcey promised Nova he would do his best to find the beast for her.

Still, it was the watches that remained the most tedious parts of each day. By the second week, Darcey went so far as to try to draw the Simerians out about their own private lives.

They answered him politely enough, but they might have been speaking code for all the sense their words possessed. They told him of hivelives and hivemates, sharemen and oneones. Even when these words seemed to possess some definite meaning as constructs, they were used in contexts that tended to invalidate any best guess. Despite this gap in communication, Darcey eventually developed a vague picture of Simerian life. The planet itself was a water world, dotted with several dozen large islands, upon each of which lived a single Simerian settlement. The problem set in when Darcey realized that the Simerians thought of each of these settlements (hives) as individual entities. When the Simerians referred to someone as "I," they might mean themselves or they might mean the hundred thousand or so other bodies who composed their own hive. Worse was when Darcey questioned the Simerians about their philosophical beliefs. In time —Darcey first struggled with the Simerian vocabulary—he understood that the Simerians considered existence to be a sort of dream thought up by the slumbering brain of their own communal hive. The *Arjuna* wasn't real. Neither was grayspace nor Darcey himself. For some reason, this view of the universe deeply irritated Darcey. He argued angrily against it. Once he went so far as to assert that the Simerians had it backward: he was the dreamer and they were the characters of his imagination.

The Simerians laughed at this. "You humans are too fantastic to be accepted except as characters in another's dream."

After this, Darcey decided the Simerians were merely joking with him. But he never could be sure.

On another occasion, Darcey mentioned the grayspace beast.

Strangely, the Simerians—who so far as he knew had never mentioned the subject before—were positive of their response. "It will exist," they said.

"It does."

They nodded. "Yes, and will."

"You've seen it?" asked Darcey, recalling his own first experience with the viewscreens and assuming that this was something similar.

"Yes."

"When? Just now? Last watch?"

"Oh, many onelives past."

A onelife, Darcey had come to understand, represented approximately one hundred common years, the apparent lifespan of an average Simerian. "But that can't be you," he said.

"Oh, yes, me."

"Your hivemates." Gradually, he had picked up many of

their words. A hivemate could be living or dead; the difference seemed insignificant to the Simerians.

"Yes, a hivemate—me."

"And he—they—you were told of it."

"And saw it."

The conversation reminded Darcey of too many in the past. In an attempt to cut through the semantic tangle, he asked, "Why don't you describe it to me, then? The beast, I mean."

"Oh, that is easily done." The Simerians actually smiled—a rare gesture for them. "The grayspace beast is that part of the hive that can be cherished but never loved." In unison, they nodded.

"I meant a physical description," Darcey said plaintively. He was hoping for additional information he might share with Commander Kaypack. "How did it look?"

"The same."

"No, look." He controlled his temper, trying to remember that his words and attitudes were no doubt as strange to them as theirs were to him. "The size and shape. The color. It was silver, wasn't it?"

The Simerians appeared confused.

"Wait," said Darcey, struck by an insight. "It isn't real, is it? The beast. It's just part of the hivedream."

But on this point the Simerians were unusually adamant: "Oh, no, it is very, very real."

Darcey gave up after that.

During the time when he was neither standing watch nor sleeping, Darcey often worked closely with Helsing, and the two of them shared the general labor of preparing the charts necessary for each day's journey. The science of grayspace navigation was more properly termed an art. Since nothing existed in grayspace, the ship's course was plotted purely on the basis of the blind laws of motion, which tended more often than not to function in grayspace as well as normal space. The one great difference lay in the matter of the lightspeed barrier. Grayspace apparently existed concurrently with normal space, but because it was a vacuum, containing neither matter nor light, velocities well in excess of the speed of light were easily attained. At the present moment, according to Helsing's figures, the *Arjuna* was traveling at a velocity one hundred twelve times that of light, but this figure, impressive as it was, had little meaning here.

Often, because of their conflicting schedules, Helsing joined Darcey in the control room during Darcey's watch. It was during one of these times, when Darcey and Helsing stood bent over a table on which were several charts, that one of the Simerians approached and laid a hand upon Darcey's shoulder.

Surprised at the touch, Darcey spun around, curiously.

The Simerian silently pointed to the rear viewscreen.

Darcey looked.

In the screen, he saw the grayspace beast.

Its silver, glistening form occupied a corner of the viewscreen.

Darcey blinked—once, twice.

The beast remained.

The Simerian said, "It is that portion of the hive that must be cherished without love."

Helsing said, "Good God, it's real!"

This was enough for Darcey. His eyes still fixed to the screen, he reached for the ship's communicator. At the last moment, he paused. "No," he said softly to himself.

Misunderstanding, Helsing said, "No, it's real—I can see it."

"Go," Darcey told the Simerians. The beast moved. It drew closer. The motion was over in the flick of an eye, but it had happened. "Fetch Kaypack and hurry. Tell him it's the beast—the grayspace beast."

"Yes, Darcey." The Simerians hurried toward the door. Even they, Darcey noted with satisfaction, had difficulty removing their eyes from the vision that filled the screen.

"And the others." Darcey pursued the Simerians to the door. "Don't tell them. Maria and Welch especially—don't say a word."

"Yes, Darcey."

He opened the door, peered down the length of the empty corridor, then ushered the Simerians out. When they had gone, Darcey shut and locked the door.

"You can't try to keep this a secret," said Helsing, accusingly. He had drawn a stray chair close to the viewscreen and now sat with his nose nearly touching the image of the silver beast. "They have a right to know, too."

"I'll let Commander Kaypack decide that."

"But he'll want to attack—to kill this . . . this . . ." Helsing seemed unable to find a word that fit his meaning.

"He is the commander," Darcey said.

"But it'll kill us. Look at that . . . that thing. My God, it's the size of a planet."

"I just think it's up to Commander Kaypack to decide."

The sight of the beast had nearly mesmerized Helsing. Even when speaking to Darcey, he never managed to make his eyes break free of the screen. "I am your superior," he said softly. "You're only an assistant navigator. I could order you to notify the others."

"I wouldn't do it," Darcey said softly.

Helsing bit his hand. "Oh, God, it's moving again. It's coming closer!"

"Well, it's about time,". said a boy. I had decided to pause briefly, knowing they were undoubtedly bursting with comments.

"What do you mean by that?" I asked. "You don't expect me to tell the story faster than it happened."

"Heck, no," said a girl (one of my favorites for a change— as devout as the color blue), "but you've got to admit you've padded things lately. What was all that bull about the Simerians for? And Nova still bitches about Kaypack, so what? The story's supposed to be about the grayspace beast, not Nova, the scrubperson."

"Well, you've got your beast now," I commented.

"Besides, it's obvious what he intended," said a boy. I slapped my ears a couple of times to keep them from telling lies. What could this be? Not a defender. The boy went on: "First, he was fulfilling some promises. He told us he'd explain more fully about the Simerians, and he did. Second, it was build-up. You don't just materialize the beast and let him growl. You have to work up to it gradually."

"Not if you don't underestimate your audience." This was that same girl again—my former favorite. "We don't need to be babied."

"I don't think" the boy began.

"No, wait," I said, enjoying myself but seeing no end. "This isn't exactly what I expected. Haven't any of you noticed? The beast—they've seen it. Helsing has seen it. Dull, drab, rational, mathematical Johann Helsing."

"Yeah—so what?"

"So what?" I felt myself growing red again. Ah, the rewards of being a guide. "It means the beast is real—that's what. It does exist."

"So?" The boy shrugged. "We knew that all along."

It may have taken next to forever for the Simerians to return with Commander Kaypack, but even if it did, Darcey failed to notice. The beast gripped him firmly in a bright, hypnotic sway. He crouched on the floor beside Helsing and barely budged his eyes.

The grayspace beast bore no certain shape. It was not circular in form as he had always anticipated, but rather more egg-shaped, but the more he watched it, the more he was sure that not even this shape remained firm for long. No, the beast flowed, expanding and contracting, pulsing like a beating heart; the edges blurred, grew indistinct, disappeared. The color was indeed silver, a hard, sharp shade, like keenly polished metal. There were no appendages, no organs of sight, touch, or sound. The beast glistened, and, Darcey was sure, it knew the ship was there.

When the door banged open, Kaypack entered alone. Stopping short, seeing Darcey and Helsing and where they were staring, he turned his eyes to the viewscreen. He saw the grayspace beast. "Oh, God," he said, dropping to the floor. "No, no, no."

"But, sir, it's the beast." Standing at last, Darcey went to lock the door. "We've found it."

"I see." Softly.

"But aren't you glad?"

"I'm not sure."

"Aren't we going to kill it?"

Kaypack peered at his palms as though the answer might somehow lie there. "How?" he asked plaintively.

"I think we better run and run fast," said Helsing.

Kaypack managed to ignore this. "It's not coming any closer," he observed.

"Sometimes it seems to and sometimes it doesn't." Darcey felt better now. Kaypack seemed stronger. "I think"—he hesitated only a moment, "I think it's watching us."

Kaypack nodded. "I think you're right."

"Then hadn't we better run?" said Helsing. "Commander, that—that thing could kill us."

"Or we could kill it," said Kaypack. A growing note of determination entered his tone.

"We can't do that!" cried Helsing.

"But we have to try." Kaypack stood up and moved to the control panel. Briefly, he studied the instruments. "It's going to move," he said. "It'll either come closer or go away. When it moves we have to be ready. Johann."

"Yes, sir." He spoke haltingly, cleaning his spectacles.

"Get away from that screen and get over here." Kaypack pointed to a chair fronting the control panel.

"What for?"

"Get over here and I'll tell you."

Helsing came unwillingly. His feet seemed to drag. At last, reaching the indicated chair, he sat with a flop. Swiveling his head, he peered at the beast.

"No," said Kaypack. "Here—not there." He touched a dial on the instrument panel. "Watch this—and watch closely. It's our velocity. If the beast changes course and we have to go after it, I don't intend to get lost in here. At any given moment I want you to be certain you can find our way back to this point. Do you understand me? I'm holding you responsible."

Helsing still seemed unable not to look at the beast, but he said, "I understand."

"And me, sir?" said Darcey.

"Lock the door."

"I already have."

"The others can't get through?"

"Not unless they break it down." The control room door was made of heavy steel. "And I don't think they can do that."

"Good." Kaypack's fingers tapped a pattern across the control panel. A moment later, Veador's face appeared in the rear viewscreen.

"Yes, my commander." Veador's voice sounded from inside the panel.

"Any problems down there?" Kaypack asked.

"No, sir," Veador said. There was no emotion in his voice —a cold, smooth tone.

"We may have to stretch things a bit in a moment."

"Yes, my commander, I know. They told me."

"The Simerians?"

"Yes, sir."

"They're there?"

"Yes." The view in the rear screen changed somewhat. Darcey saw the Simerians standing behind Veador.

"It's the beast, Veador."

"They told me that."

"It's real."

"Yes, sir."

"I'll be in voice contact with you."

"Yes, my commander."

"I don't think he's frightened at all," Kaypack told Darcey in a softer tone.

"He hasn't seen it."

"No," Kaypack said, glancing surreptitiously at the screen that showed the beast. "That's true."

A sharp rapping sounded at the outer door. Helsing moved from his seat as if to answer.

Kaypack said, "Sit down."

A muffled voice penetrated the door. Darcey recognized it as Rickard Welch's. "Kaypack, open up in there. We know what you're up to. Let us in."

Kaypack said, "Veador, I'm going to accelerate slightly."

From the control panel: "Yes, my commander."

Kaypack's fingers tapped. He jerked a long steel lever. Darcey looked at the viewscreen: the beast had grown.

"Kaypack!" cried a shrill voice. Maria. "Let us in there, you crazy fool!"

Darcey stared at the screen. There was no sense of increased motion, but the image of the beast swelled and swelled. Its silver glistening bulk filled a third of the screen . . . half of it . . . all of it. . . .

"We're going to hit!" he cried in sudden terror.

"Yes," said Kaypack softly.

Both were wrong. As suddenly as it had grown, the beast began to shrink. It filled half the screen, then only a quarter.

"I thought so," Kaypack said. "It's running. Veador!" he called.

"Yes, my commander."

"I'm going to double our velocity."

"We're ready, sir."

From outside the door: "Kaypack, damn you, Kaypack!"

Helsing, his body trembling, hands shaking, stared at the instrument panel.

The beast was now no larger than when it had originally appeared.

"It can't go this fast!" Kaypack said. He banged the controls in front of him. "It's impossible—it can't!"

"My commander," came Veador's voice, "I don't believe we can attain any higher velocity without seriously endangering the drive."

"Faster!" cried Kaypack. "We must go faster!"

"Yes, my commander."

"Kaypack, open up in there. What are you doing? For God's sake, answer us."

Darcey peered at the viewscreen. The beast was no larger than a nearby star seen in normal space, and even as he watched, it continued to shrink. They were involved in a race for life, he knew, and they were being beaten as easily as a man might outrun a laboring insect.

"That thing!" Kaypack was saying. "What is it? How can it possibly—?"

Something groaned. The ship quivered as if caught in the grip of some monstrous fist. Darcey, leaving his feet, slammed hard against the floor. He felt Helsing pile on top of him and heard the whine of a voice raised in terror. Dimly recognizing Helsing, he refused to feel any sympathy, but then a shrieking, grinding, moaning sound drowned all his thoughts. Darcey heard his own voice screaming. He was lifted bodily into the air and slammed down. This happened once, twice, then again.

At last: utter silence.

Darcey vaguely understood that the *Arjuna* was not moving.

"We're ruined," said Helsing, who lay on top of Darcey.

"Get off me."

"Oh. Sorry."

Darcey slowly struggled to his feet. He blinked his eyes and shook his aching head in astonishment.

The control room was an utter mess. All four viewscreens lay scattered upon the floor. An ugly, acrid smoke filled the air.

Kaypack, who had miraculously retained his footing, stared at the wreckage surrounding him. "I can't believe it," he said gently. "It's impossible—I can't." One of his fists opened and shut with an irregular, spasmodic rhythm.

Maria's voice from beyond the door: "Kaypack? Are you alive in there? Answer me if you can!"

"Should I let her in?" Darcey asked.

But Helsing, without being asked, went over and opened the door.

Maria entered first, then Nova, then Welch. Except for Welch, whose lip was bleeding, they seemed unharmed.

Kaypack stared at them without apparent recognition. He was shaking his head.

"You idiot!" said Welch. "You damn near killed us. What a stupid, senseless . . ." Charging across the room, he came straight at Kaypack.

It occurred so swiftly that Darcey never saw the blow. Kaypack swung casually from his heels. A second later, Welch collapsed.

Kaypack hurried toward the door.

"Commander Kaypack," Darcey said hesitantly. "Sir, shouldn't I—?"

Kaypack paused halfway out the door. "Until I return, assume command," he said.

It was impossible to determine whom he meant.

Then he was gone.

I believed I had succeeded in impressing them at last. When I finished, nobody let out a peep.

Finally, I spoke. "Well, what do you think?"

"I think," said one student, "Kaypack has a hell of a problem."

"How so?"

"How can he kill the beast if he can't catch it?"

"That," I said, "is undoubtedly one problem that's worrying him right now."

"And even if he did catch it," said another, "what could he do? The thing is so huge, so powerful. How can he hope even to dent it?"

"And that," I said, "is the other problem."

FOUR

By this time I realized they were glaring at me in mass. "What's the problem?" I asked, divertingly.

Their spokesman proved to be a boy I would not have chosen myself. "We've been talking."

"I gathered that."

"And we feel we've got a right to know."

"Perhaps you do."

"What's the point of all this?"

I fingered my chin whiskers as though his question had thrown me for a square loop (which of course it had not). "Now that's moving into the area of the purpose of art," I said, artfully, "and each of you has had a barrel of guff on the subject. I don't see why I should be expected to explain what should be obvious."

"Didactic."

He amazed me. "You think so?"

A firm, youthful nod. "We all do. You've never told us a story this long. It's got to have a point. A purpose. So give."

"Okay."

During the period in which Commander Kaypack remained secluded behind the firm barrier of his stateroom door, a mood of pure confusion gripped the crew. In spite of this, twice a day, as regular as the expansion of the universe,

Darcey and Nova appeared at the locked door. Nova always carried a tray of food.

"Hey, what's this?"

I glanced up. Disarmingly. "It's what you wanted."

"The hell if it is. That's just more of the dumb story."

"Exactly," I said.

"We asked for the point."

"And you're going to get it." I chuckled, then went on.

Darcey knocked. "Commander Kaypack, it's us. Please open up. We've brought food."

There was never a reply.

"Sir, we've tried to repair the drive but it's no use. We're stalled."

No answer.

Nova spoke with anger: "Kaypack, this is your dinner out here. I swear I'll take it away and eat it myself if you don't open up."

Silence.

Darcey murmured, "I hope he hasn't suffered any illness or injury."

"That old fool?"

"He could be dead."

"You know better than that. He's thinking in there—that's what he's doing. He's thinking about that big, bad beast he chased and how the hell he's going to get himself out of this mess."

Darcey shook his head. "What mess?"

"Never mind." Nova struck the heavy door with two clanging fists. "I'm giving you till three to open up, Kaypack. I mean it. One . . . two . . . three . . ."

The door did not open.

"You bastard!"

They departed, minus the tray of food.

Later in the day (or the next day), when they returned, the tray was gone.

"The sly old sneak," said Nova.

Darcey knocked. "Commander Kaypack, it's us. Please open up. We've brought food."

There was never a reply.

As Darcey honestly reported to Kaypack, the grayspace drive was broken and nobody knew how to repair it. Veador had spent three days in a vain attempt before finally giving up. The Simerians watched him all the time. When Veador turned away at last, they said, "We see where the problem is."

Veador spluttered angrily, but Darcey said, "Then won't you fix it?"

"Kaypack is our commander."

"He's mine, too," said Veador, glaring.

"Without his direct order, it would not be proper for us to proceed."

Veador called them liars but Darcey wasn't so sure. After the chase, as soon as he caught up with them in the crew quarters, Darcey asked the Simerians, "Why did you tell? I asked you not to, but Nova says you told her and you must have told Welch and Maria, too."

The Simerians nodded in unison, slender jaws bobbing as if on a taut string. "They asked us."

"But you didn't have to tell them."

The Simerians shrugged. They seemed to make a practice of adopting human gestures. "Are they not characters, too?"

Darcey felt his face flush with anger. "No, damn it, they're people."

Two matching toothless grins. "All the more reason to tell them, don't you agree?"

"No!" But Darcey was never quite sure of that.

During the period of Kaypack's seclusion and Veador's fruitless labors, Welch and Maria remained strangely quiescent. Once for several hours they holed up alone with Helsing in the ship's lounge, and Nova said she thought she knew what was up.

"They aren't going to believe you or Kaypack. He's crazy and you're damn near an alien, but Helsing scares them. He saw the beast! The dullest, most narrow-minded little man on fourteen planets and he saw it!"

"He did, too," said Darcey.

"And that's the point. Welch and Maria want to get him to change his mind and decide he didn't."

But when the three of them emerged, Darcey could tell by the bleakness of their expressions that Helsing had not been convinced. The little man lived in a universe in which the human senses, even when mechanically extended through viewscreen projection, were incapable of telling lies; he believed his eyes before he believed his own rational mind.

Maria at least came halfway to believing. She sighed. "Either way, Darcey, it was a crazy thing for Kaypack to do. You were there—you tell me. What was on his mind? Was he going to chase the beast till he caught it, then ram the fiend with the bow of the cruiser? If what Helsing says is true, the beast is incredibly huge and powerful. Does a bug go chasing after a man?"

Darcey tried to draw himself up with dignity. In the absence of Kaypack, he alone could explain. "I don't think the commander believes he is a bug."

"Not a bug," said Welch, giggling, "but bugs. Even the stellar code, which I assume applies to us, permits a crew to replace its commander when and if he loses possession of sufficient good judgment to operate the ship in such a way as not to unnecessarily damage the lives of those to whom he is responsible. In my opinion, that's exactly the painful situation we now face." Welch, finishing, glanced surreptitiously around the crowded crew quarters, his little eyes leaping quickly from face to face, plainly seeking agreement.

But none of them—not even Maria—was presently prepared to relieve Kaypack of command. Their mutual impotence in the face of current disaster caused them to doubt their own native abilities. After all, even if he was bugs, Kaypack still could lead, and that was more than anyone else could presently claim.

Welch heaved a disappointed sigh. "I wish he'd come out of that room," he said.

But it was Nova who concerned Darcey the most, because it was only her opinion, he was frank to admit, that he really valued.

On the third day of Kaypack's hibernation, as they returned from his stateroom, Darcey finally found the nerve to pop the question. The high corridor rang with the sound of their pounding bootheels. "Nova, do you think I saw the beast?"

She shook her head and answered carefully, "I'm not sure I've made up my mind."

"But how can you say that?" He knew he was speaking too loudly; he had waited too long to ask the question. "Either I saw it or I didn't."

"Maybe you saw something else."

"But that's ridiculous. This is grayspace—nothing lives here except the beast."

She shrugged. "Are you sure? Welch will tell you that nothing lives here period. If you want to make an exception for the beast, why can't I make another exception for something else?"

"You just don't want to say one way or the other."

She smiled. "You know, I think you're right. Look, Darcey, I've lived in a lot of different places and seen a lot of different things, but I've never seen a grayspace beast. Now it's pretty crazy to think you and Helsing and the Simerians and Kaypack all went goony at the same moment, but it's also pretty crazy to think there's such a thing as a grayspace beast." She held up a hand to halt his attempted interruption. "But I believe you. And I'll tell you why, too. It's something the others don't know about, but Veador does, and I think he believes, too, for the same reason. Darcey, do you remember that very first night when I tried to waylay you inside the concession?"

"Sure, I remember."

"And what happened?"

"It didn't work—Kaypack stopped you."

"And why didn't it work? Don't you remember? It didn't work because you weren't fooled. All that expensive illusion, and all you saw was what was there."

"That's right—so what?"

"So I don't think you can be fooled. For a minute maybe, you can make a mistake like anyone, but you aren't really capable of seeing what isn't there. Kaypack knows that. I think your aliens—the Radians—trained you to be that way, just so you could do what you're doing now. Why do you think Kaypack's so scared he's hiding in his stateroom and won't come out?"

"He's not scared," said Darcey.

"Because he knows what you saw was true. Hell, he'd never believe himself any more than the rest of us would—but he knows you can't see a lie. So, yes, I believe you. What else can I do?"

"But you said it might not be the beast."

She grinned. "That's my way of staying sane."

At the end of five days, Kaypack emerged from his stateroom at last. When he entered the control room, only Darcey and Nova were present. Nova worked fitfully with a broom, sweeping shards of broken glass into neat piles. Darcey, sprawled in a chair beside the main control panel, viewed her work with interest.

When Kaypack entered, both looked up in shock.

"Sir, you're here," cried Darcey, stating the rather obvious.

"It's the return of the grayspace ranger," Nova said, with a mocking smile of apparent pleasure.

Kaypack didn't repond. He carried a small tool kit under one arm, and without a word to the others, he went over to the control panel, crouched down, and set a wide screwdriver to work.

Darcey looked at Nova and she at him. Neither seemed to have any solution to this puzzle.

Finally, snapping the spell of irresolution, Darcey marched over to Kaypack's side and stood stiffly over him. "Sir, any orders you wish to relate to us?"

"Oh, Darcey." Kaypack looked up from the work below with apparent surprise. Darcey noted a deeper hollowness in the commander's eyes, and there was a certain new paleness to his face. Darcey had somehow expected a dramatic transformation. What he now saw disappointed him. Wasn't the beast more crucial than this?

"There must be something we can do, sir."

Kaypack flashed a weary smile. "I think not, Darcey. Let's get the ship to functioning again and then see. You've done an excellent job cleaning up the damage."

"That was me, Kaypack," said Nova, sauntering over. "I'm your serf—remember?"

"Oh, yes, Nova. The shell game." He acted as though he might actually have forgotten.

"Sir, do you mean you think you can repair the damage?"

"Oh, sure. If I didn't, we'd be in a pack of trouble, right?" He replaced the screwdriver inside the tool kit, then inserted a wrench within the control-panel wreckage. The wrench made a sharp, whirring noise as it set invisibly to work.

"Welch thinks we imagined the beast, sir."

"Oh, yes, the grayspace beast." Kaypack appeared to be studying the work of the tool, though nothing could actually be seen. Nova crouched down beside him, grinning as she pretended to be watching, too.

"He's threatening to relieve you of command."

"Welch is?"

"Yes, sir. He thinks you're crazy."

Kaypack smiled in private bemusement. "He may be right."

"I'm beginning to think so," said Nova. She pointed to the opening where the wrench was whirring. "What's so interesting in there?"

Kaypack shook his head but reached inside and removed the wrench. "Nothing now—it's fixed." He stood up.

Darcey intercepted him at the door. "Where are you going now, sir?"

"The engine room. I have to fix the drive, don't I?" He smiled faintly.

"But what about the beast, sir?"

Kaypack shook his head. "What about it? It's gone, isn't it? If you're curious, activate the viewscreens. They should be working again."

"But are we going to chase it or what?"

"We can't." That faint, distant smile again. "We don't know where it is."

"But aren't we going to look?"

Kaypack, for the first time, spoke with some conviction. "We aren't," he said.

"But we have to!"

Kaypack faced Darcey's anger without flinching. "Because of the Radians?"

"Yes. They gave us the ship for that."

The faint smile reappeared. "Then let them come and take it away."

Kaypack went out the door.

Confused and frantic, Darcey spun around to face Nova, who stood with a hand resting on the control panel and a look on her face that said, *see, what did I tell you?* "He's scared," she said.

"No, he's not," said Darcey. Spinning again, he hurried out after Kaypack. There was no other place to go.

After three long days of unceasing labor in the engine room with only Veador to help him, Kaypack gathered the crew in the ship's lounge to announce that the *Arjuna* was once again prepared to resume its normal course. "Helsing tells me," said Kaypack, "that it'll take us five days at normal cruising speed to reach the point where we diverted from our course. I'm sorry for the delay, but it's too late to do anything about that. So, starting now, we'll resume our regular watches."

If Kaypack had had his way, the meeting would have ended there. Welch sprang to his feet and called on Kaypack to stay put. "I don't think that settles it," he said.

"Why?" said Kaypack. "Do you have another alternative, Rickard?"

"Yes. I want to know what's going on. So does Maria. So do all of us."

Kaypack shrugged. The mood of detachment he had brought with him from his stateroom exile had in no way lessened. "We're going back the way we came."

"And this thing? This beast?"

"Why?" Kaypack tilted a curious brow. "Have you seen it?"

"No, of course not." Plainly striving to keep his anger at a high pitch, Welch was experiencing considerable difficulty in the face of Kaypack's soft serenity. "I want to know what you intend to do if we do."

"Nothing," said Kaypack.

Welch seemed disappointed as well as surprised. He struggled for a long moment to get out a word, but Maria interrupted before he could manage.

"Kail, may we have your word on that?"

Kaypack acted surprised to find everyone so adamant. "My word on what?" As though he had forgotten.

"Your word that you won't go chasing after any grayspace beasts unless the rest of us agree."

"You've got it," said Kaypack.

"Your word?"

"Yes."

Darcey, listening to this with controlled silence, felt a pit of emptiness and sorrow gaping in his belly.

"If there are no other questions," Kaypack said, "I'll head up to the control room." He moved alone toward the door. Pausing briefly, he added, "Oh, Helsing, once the ship's under way I'd like to see you alone for a few moments."

Helsing acted surprised. "What about?"

"Oh, I'll tell you at the time." Kaypack shrugged. "Merely some points of navigation."

At this point I finally received some of the cries I had been long expecting. "Hey, wait a minute!" was the gist of most of them.

So I waited a minute. "There's something you don't understand?"

"Yes," said a boy, not their previous spokesman, for which I was thankful. "I don't understand what all this is about. You mean Kaypack has given up on the beast already? That doesn't make sense."

He had said exactly what I'd been hoping for. With satisfied pleasure, I crossed my hands upon my belly. "But that's exactly what it does make. Look, we're all agreed by now that Kaypack didn't really expect to find the grayspace beast and when he did it scared him out of two hundred years worth of life. What was worse, when he went chasing after it, the beast made him look like a bug battling a grown man, and if that didn't scare him more, then it certainly did make him hesitant. He spent five days alone in his stateroom. What do you think he was doing all that time?"

"Thinking," was the obvious response.

"Good, but what about?"

"Why, about how to chase and kill the beast, what else?"

"And what did he decide?"

"Well, according to you, that he ought to just forget about the whole thing and go back to making money."

"I never said that. Kaypack did."

"What's the difference?" said a voice from the back, but I wasn't about to be lured into another discussion concerning my own identity. I waited patiently until a marvelous girl finally got around to saying what should have been plain to them all:

"I suppose, in a way, he didn't have much choice. If he'd come to them and said we're going after the beast, he might have had a mutiny on his hands."

"Or at least a pack of discontent?" I prodded. "And fear?"

She nodded. "At least."

"And we still haven't answered my first question, have we? If Kaypack is going to chase the beast, then what's he going to do if he catches it? How many of you think he's solved that problem?"

Two hands went up, and I pointed randomly at the nearest. "Then tell me what it is."

He laughed uncomfortably. "How should I know?"

"Then how should Kaypack know?"

"He's smarter than me."

"So am I—but I don't know."

"Then—"

I had led them far enough already. "I'll give you one last hint. How did this section end?"

"With Kaypack on his way to start the drive."

"No, no." These were the same children who had been taught since birth about the power of human concentration. "At the very end?"

A bright child (girl): "Kaypack told Johann Helsing he wanted to see him in private."

"And what's Helsing's position aboard the *Arjuna?*"

"Navigator." Nearly all of them could answer that one.

"And what does a navigator do?" I felt like I was teaching a first session again.

"He navigates." That from one of my dimmer pupils.

"He plots the course the ship must follow to reach its proper destination."

That would suffice. "Now you're getting the idea," I said,

as though the cosmic equation had been recomputed in my presence. "Now back to the story."

"Hey, wait, you forgot—"

They'd had their minute. I bulled onward.

A few hours after the *Arjuna* was again under way, Kaypack entered the control room. Darcey had agreed to serve first watch with the Simerians, and the three of them sat alone. The four big viewscreens showed varying visions of empty grayspace.

"No beast, I see," said Kaypack, seating himself in an empty chair beside Darcey. He easily ignored the presence of the silent, cuddling Simerians. "I don't expect we'll see it again this time."

"No, sir," said Darcey, softly and politely. "That way we won't have to run away."

Kaypack nodded, apparently unhurt although Darcey had intended to wound him. "And that's what we will do if it's necessary. We'll run."

In spite of a silent vow not to make himself vulnerable again, Darcey could not resist asking, "But why, sir?"

"To protect our necks," Kaypack said without hesitation.

"But then you lied to me."

Kaypack scratched his chin. By now, Darcey knew this was the gesture he made use of when he wanted someone to think he was thinking. "Actually, that's a point I've had to consider, and to tell the truth, I don't know. Darcey, I didn't believe in the beast. Maybe I should have—the elders wouldn't make such a mistake—but I wanted so badly to get back into space."

"You're like Welch and Maria. You want to make money."

Kaypack laughed mockingly, more at himself than at Darcey. "I don't think you believe that's true."

"Then tell me what is true," Darcey said pleadingly. "You ought to know—it's you we're talking about."

"Then the truth is that we're weak, impotent, uncertain.

The elders sent us out to kill the beast without bothering to tell us why or how. Darcey, that wasn't fair. It erases any obligation I might owe them."

"Then you're just going to go on as if it never happened?"

"Until I find a way."

"And how are you going to do that?"

"By asking them."

Darcey felt as if he had somehow been left lingering far behind by a fleet, thinking speedster. "You're going to ask the elders?"

"I just had a talk with Helsing. He's going to prepare new charts, revising our course. I didn't tell him. I said I'd come across a more promising star. But that star's the one that shines over Radius, Darcey, and it's where we're going."

Darcey wanted to let out a big cheer. "I knew you'd say that, sir. I knew it all along."

Kaypack let the obvious pass without comment. "Don't let your hopes rise too high. I said I'd ask them. That's all I can do. Maybe they don't know. Maybe they won't say."

"But don't you think they do?"

"When I climbed Gorgan Mount, there was something there—something I saw or felt or noticed—and I can't get the feeling out of my mind. Whatever it was, it has something to do with the beast. Remember, the Radians built their own cruisers thousands of years before men came down from the trees. They know enough about the beast to want it dead, and they care enough about the danger to train you from birth to help in accomplishing that. The elders must know something, but they may not want to tell."

"And if they don't? If they won't?"

"Then it's over, Darcey," Kaypack said bluntly.

"You won't go on?"

"I won't risk the lives of everyone on this ship. Their lives and their sanity. If the elders want the *Arjuna* back, I'll give it to them. But I won't come out here again."

Darcey nodded slowly. "I think you're right, sir."
Kaypack smiled. "Thank you, Darcey."

"I've been noticing something odd." Another unsolicited interruption. "You're telling the story differently now."
I had been wondering if anyone would ever get around to noticing. I'd been feeling like a gorgeous woman in a gorgeous gown stuck in a room full of blind men. "How so?"
"Well, in the beginning you used a variety of points of view. You started with Kaypack and there was Darcey on Radius and then Nova and even Veador. Once, if I remember, you used the entire crew, one after the other, Maria and Helsing and the Simerians."
"I'd never use the Simerians," I said, shivering. "To show you their thoughts I'd have to talk gibberish."
"Well, the others, then."
I nodded. "That's right."
"But lately—I can't remember from exactly when—it's been all Darcey."
"Since they escaped from Paradise Planet," a student added.
"No, since before then—from the time the crew was hired. The escape was all Darcey, too."
"Well, so what?" I said.
"Isn't it kind of odd? I mean, Kaypack's the protagonist more than Darcey. Like just now you spent ten minutes telling us how Kaypack told Darcey what was in his mind. If Kaypack was the point of view, you could have just told us his mind and skipped the entire conversation."
"That's right. I could have if I'd wanted."
"And"—this was one of my loveliest girls—"you gave us only a secondhand account, and hardly any of that, of the conversation between Kaypack and Helsing. To me, that would have been a lot more interesting than what we got. I mean, what exactly did Kaypack tell him, how did he lie, how much did Helsing figure out?"

"Yeah, that's right."

"That's true."

"What's up, old man?"

Like a pack of wolves, they mauled the bait—me. I grinned at them. "So there's only one conclusion," I said.

"You're a lousy storyteller."

"Or . . ." I said, leadingly.

"Or Kaypack isn't the protagonist anymore—it's Darcey."

I could have kissed the brain behind that insight.

At Kaypack's urging, Darcey said nothing to anyone of their sudden change of course. If the others suspected any-thing—even Helsing—they gave no obvious hints. Kaypack passed the word that he'd discovered a more promising star, and that word was accepted without question. Darcey real-ized that Kaypack, through subterfuge, had managed to be-come a leader again.

Darcey worried only about the Simerians, who had over-heard his conversation with Kaypack, but the commander insisted he need have no fear on that point. "They wouldn't think of breathing a word to anyone."

"They told Welch and Maria about the beast."

"Sure, but that's different. They did that for the reason they do everything—added excitement, to juice up the dream. If they told now, Welch would simply shove me aside and take command. It's the same reason they refused to repair the broken drive. The more exciting the dream, the longer they can go without waking up."

The one person Darcey wanted to tell but couldn't was Nova. He even went so far as to ask Kaypack if it wasn't all right, but Kaypack, perhaps recalling Nova's initial treach-ery, said no.

"But I'm sure we can trust her," Darcey insisted. "Didn't you give her your money to hold back on Paradise Planet?"

"Sure, and I didn't say I didn't trust her. I said I didn't see any reason why we should."

Darcey had to agree with that and so he kept his lips firmly sealed—even with Nova.

A dozen common days after Kaypack successfully repaired the broken drive, the *Arjuna*, without incident, jumped back into normal space. The Radian sun, a tiny yellow stain of flickering light, burned in the center of the forward viewscreen. Even though he'd never before viewed the star under which he'd been born from such a perspective, Darcey was strangely moved by the sight. He experienced a tightening sensation in his throat and lungs, as though gripped and squeezed by a strong hand. As the days passed and the star appeared to grow, his emotion, if anything, increased. During watches, he struggled to look anywhere but at that steady yellow disk. He imagined that everyone else must be aware of his odd behavior, but even Nova, who spent considerable time at his side, said nothing.

When Radius itself shone as the second-brightest object in the sky and Darcey could not look at a screen without shivering and trembling, the *Arjuna* suddenly bucked and heaved to a total stall.

Darcey and the Simerians stood watch at the time, and Nova huddled nearby. A few moments after the shock, before anyone in the control room had a chance to recover, the forward viewscreen flickered and Kaypack's face replaced the Radian view. The background from which he spoke, it was plain, was the engine room.

Kaypack said, "Ladies and gentlemen of the crew, I want to assure you there's no immediate danger. The *Arjuna* has stalled at our present location, some 8.78 light-minutes from our intended destination." Darcey, checking the lighted gauges on the control panel, determined that this figure was exactly correct. "In order to discuss the situation, I want to meet with you immediately in the ship's lounge. Again, I repeat: there is no immediate danger."

Kaypack's face was replaced by an unchanging vista of star-studded space. Radius glimmered a greenish gold.

"What the hell is going on now?" said Nova. She came to her feet and glared at Darcey. "Is this another of Kaypack's silly tricks?"

"I wouldn't have any idea," Darcey said, although he did have an idea (one). Until he was sure the danger was past, he didn't intend to tell Nova anything. "Maybe we ought to go to the ship's lounge and find out."

She turned on a heel and marched instantly for the door. Darcey waited for the Simerians to follow. When neither budged, he said, "Didn't you hear what the commander said?"

They shook their heads in firm unison. "We will remain to study the situation."

"Don't you want to know what's wrong?"

"Oh, we know that already. There is no direct danger."

Darcey was tempted to ask what they knew but finally decided he could wait to hear it directly from Kaypack.

He hurried to catch up with Nova.

When they reached the lounge, the others—Welch, Maria, and Helsing—had arrived ahead of them. None had any more idea than Nova did of what might be up. Maria said they'd felt the shock, then heard the announcement, while resting in the crew quarters. "If Kaypack's done something stupid, I'll strangle him with my own hands, I swear it."

"It may be only an accident," Helsing said. In spite of these comforting words, he appeared less at ease and more fearful than anyone else present.

"And Kaypack just happened to be present in the engine room at that exact moment?" Maria said.

"He may have been attempting to repair an earlier malfunction."

"And he may have been trying to make a later, bigger one."

Welch, who had remained untypically quiet until now, said, "Why don't we simply shut up until Kaypack arrives?"

The way he said it—the lack of any feeling in his tone—convinced everyone he was correct.

A full fifteen minutes passed with no sign of Kaypack.

Twice Nova broke the silence to ask Darcey if he knew what was up.

Both times Darcey said, "I don't have any idea." He was sure he flushed when he did.

When Kaypack arrived at last, Veador bustled in his wake. From the downcast tilt of Veador's head and the blank expression on his face, Darcey decided to expect the worst. Veador slipped to the floor in front of Nova and Darcey, while Kaypack proceeded to the front of the room. The alien's tail thumped vigorously with agitation.

Kaypack spoke immediately and his tone was soft and even, as if he were relating a most commonplace series of events. "As you know, the *Arjuna* is presently stalled. I thought you'd all like to know how this came about, and it's really quite simple. I did it. I ordered Veador outside the engine room—there's no need for him to bear any of the blame—and then tampered with the fusion engine. The damage is relatively minor—it can be corrected in a few days' time—but it is technical. Except for myself and Veador, I don't think there's anyone on board who can repair it. Johann, why don't you tell them what this will mean in terms of our course?"

Before anyone had a chance to vent his feelings at what Kaypack had confessed, Helsing promptly explained, "The *Arjuna*, driven by the forces of inertia, will continue on its present course. Because of our high velocity, we ought easily to make rendezvous with the planet of our destination. I don't have the figures at hand, but I imagine we can expect to spend an additional eight or nine days getting there."

"Seven," said Kaypack.

Helsing nodded an acknowledgment. "Of course, without the added stimulus of the engine, we will, upon rendezvous, simply drift into orbit around this planet."

"Thank you, Johann," said Kaypack. "Now"—he glanced from silent face to silent face—"are there any other questions?"

This served as a signal for a variety of outbursts. Maria ranted, Nova shouted, and Welch sprang silently to his feet. In the end, it was Welch who received Kaypack's nod. "Yes, Rickard, what is it?"

"I think," Welch said softly, "we deserve some form of explanation for your conduct."

Kaypack nodded. "I agree. Darcey, I think you can explain this as well as I. Tell them where we're headed and why."

"We . . . I . . ." Darcey took a deep breath and tried to start again. "The planet where I was born is called—"

"Either speak up or stand up," Welch said gruffly. "I can't understand a word you're saying."

Bleakly, Darcey rose to his feet. Standing there, he told them everything he could about Radius, the grayspace beast, and Kaypack's intentions. "If the elders agree to tell us how to kill the beast, then we can return to grayspace and do it. If not, Commander Kaypack feels we should resume our mission as an exploratory cruiser."

"Thank you, Darcey," said Kaypack.

Gratefully, Darcey dropped down. Nova, beside him, glared with a bitter anger he could not endure.

Welch, who had remained standing, said, "I should have suspected something like this when you suddenly decided to approach this other star instead, but I'm afraid you managed to fool me before. I really believed you'd given up this crazy endeavor."

"Once a nut, always a nut," Maria said.

"Once a liar, always a liar," murmured Nova. She looked at Darcey, not Kaypack, when she said this.

"But I'm afriad," said Welch, "that none of this, as interesting as it undoubtedly is, fully explains why you've chosen to damage the ship."

"Simple enough," said Kaypack. "In a few more hours,

we're going to be close enough to Radius to begin taking atmospheric samples. A few hours after that, we can make telescopic contact. If I remember correctly from six hundred years ago, you ought not to notice anything odd until we're much closer. But I can't trust the Radians. They're strong. They may do something to draw attention to their presence. I intended, when you discovered my plans, that I, not you, would have the upper hand. I think I have that now."

Welch nodded slowly, while Maria cursed and Nova glowered. Helsing, his mouth open in a speechless oval, appeared barely cognizant of what was occurring. "I think it's safe to say you've got that now," said Welch. "I assume we can expect no assistance from Veador."

Kaypack nodded. "Tell them, Veador."

Veador said, in a deliberately neutral voice, "My commander has commanded me not to undertake any repairs except at his explicit direction."

"I suppose you had no choice in that, Veador," Welch said. Even Maria had fallen silent now; she appeared willing, at least for the moment, to let Welch speak for her.

"No," said Veador.

"Are you eager to go hunting the grayspace beast?"

"No."

"Do you think Commander Kaypack is mad?"

"I do not," said Veador. He raised his eyes at last, glanced briefly at Kaypack, then lowered them.

"Neither do I," said Welch. "This is sheer blackmail, and blackmailers—I have some past experience—are never mad."

"Thank you," said Kaypack. "Would you mind then if I stated my terms?"

"Not at all, though I imagine I can guess them."

"Why didn't you tell me?" Nova whispered during the slight pause.

Darcey turned to her. "I'm sorry—I wanted to but Kaypack said—"

Kaypack said, "In return for repairing the engine, I simply

want permission to lead a party of my choice down to the surface of Radius. When I'm finished talking to the natives, I'll return here and do what I've promised."

"We could wait you out," Welch said. "If you tried to force your way aboard a shuttle, we could stop you."

"That's why I'd rather handle it this way. I can be a very stubborn man when I want to."

"You haven't mentioned afterward. What then? Am I to believe you'll return to this ship with information describing how to kill this beast of yours and then take no further action?"

"I think that should be decided at the proper time. My information may even convince you that some things are more important than wealth."

Welch glanced slowly around the room as though counting heads. At last he said, "Will you accept a free vote of the entire crew?"

Maria laughed in sheer surprise.

"I will," said Kaypack. This time Maria gasped. "One vote for one person."

"And no votes for aliens." Welch had apparently done a better job of counting heads than Maria.

"I don't agree. Veador and the Simerians are as much a part of this crew as you or I. When the vote comes, Veador will have his own head. I'll make no attempt to command him."

"Then," said Welch, "I must insist that you and Darcey remove yourselves from the voting. If obligation is to be our measure, then I say that you are already too deeply committed to these Radians."

By this time Darcey had done his own counting. He found the Simerians and possibly Veador on Kaypack's side. Welch and Maria were adamantly opposed. Recalling Helsing's fear at the time of the chase, he included him, too. Nova made four.

But Kaypack said: "I agree to those terms."

Refusing to expose his surprise, Welch moved quickly.

Hurrying across the room, he gripped Kaypack's hand. "Then we're agreed?"

Kaypack shook hands impassively. "We're agreed."

Welch smiled, extracting his hand. He turned to Maria as though expecting a burst of applause, but she appeared less than pleased by the agreement. "I still think he's out of his mind," she said.

"Don't be a fool," Welch told her. He faced Kaypack again. "I assume Darcey will be accompanying you."

"Yes, for one."

This seemed to surprise Welch. "There'll be another?"

"Yes," said Kaypack. "Nova will be going along, too."

"Oh, no, you won't!" she cried, springing to her feet in an instant. "If you want me, it'll be dead, not alive."

Kaypack smiled at Welch. "I believe our agreement stipulated a party of my choice," he said.

Welch said, in disgust, "Nova, shut up."

"I'll shut up but I won't go."

But somehow Darcey already knew that in the end she would.

And he was right.

"Now I see it," said one bright boy. "Kaypack's already fudging the headcount."

This was one remark I had not anticipated. "What do you mean?"

"Brainwashing. The Radians will do that for him. By the time Nova returns to the ship, she'll do anything he tells her. That'll throw the vote right there."

I let out my most disgusted sigh. "Would you mind telling me," I said politely, "exactly where you heard about brainwashing? I know it wasn't from me."

He was casual. "Everybody knows about that. Mental or physical torture—it's easy."

"On you, maybe it is, but in case you haven't noticed, Nova has a good brain of her own."

"Hey, he's jealous," cried someone.

"Look," I explained, bluntly and patiently, "if brainwashing was all that easy, why should Kaypack even bother with the Radians? He could set to work on Nova's brain with his own hands, scrub it clean in a minute or two, then have his needed vote."

"It's not that easy," he said, scoffing. "The Radians have special powers. You told us that yourself. They talk to each other inside their heads."

"And you call that brainwashing?" (It was my turn to scoff.)

"No, but it's—"

"Listen," I said, smoothing and soothing my voice, "this is supposed to be a school, which means our duty is to teach. Now, if brainwashing was such a common practice, why should we go through all the trouble we do trying to put things inside your thick heads, when we could simply take each of you aside and practice some mental or physical torture until you were ripe and then stuff a wad of enlightenment into your brains? If you think the Radians are powerful, then I believe you're underestimating the staff of this institution."

"But not you," said a girl.

While they chuckled, I smiled myself, knowing I'd scored my points. "Meanwhile back on Radius," I said, reclaiming their attention at once.

The shuttle touched down at the edge of the sea, and Kaypack said this was the same spot where he himself had first landed six centuries before. Even before Kaypack had thrust open the forward hatch, Darcey, peeping through a side window, had spotted Sung standing motionlessly among the first spreading trees of the inland forest.

"How did he know?" Darcey said, reaching anxiously forward and clutching hold of Kaypack's arm.

"Don't ask." Kaypack thrust open the forward hatch. "It'll only get you a headache."

Because Sung had in no way changed physically, Darcey further anticipated that the elder's firm silence would also remain unaltered. Therefore, Darcey felt deeply astonished when, as he and Kaypack and Nova crossed the sand, Sung came running to meet them. He waved an angry fist above his head and opened his lips in a series of angry, frantic exclamations.

"Uh-oh," said Kaypack. "This is worse than I'd thought."

"He's angry," said Darcey, still surprised.

"I'd say so, too."

Reaching the three humans, Sung stopped in the moist sand and thrust a finger at Darcey. "You were directed never to return to this world. You have betrayed us, Darcey."

"I didn't think—"

"And you," Sung said, swiveling to face Kaypack, "also promised not to return. You swore never to reveal the location or existence of our world and yet you have come with a full ship."

"I came because I had to," Kaypack said evenly.

"And yet you lied."

"I came because you were stupid."

Sung showed his shock. "Don't be absurd."

"You sent Darcey to me with certain instructions and at the same time refused to grant me enough information to carry out those instructions. If that's not stupid, Sung, I don't know what is."

"You were told what was necessary for you to know. We gave you your ship. We gave you money."

"I can't kill the grayspace beast by throwing money at it."

Sung caught his breath. "You have seen this beast?"

"I have."

"And you fled?" It was an accusation.

"It did—not us."

"You pursued?"

"We tried—the beast won the race."

"Then it fears you," said Sung.

Kaypack shook his head. "Now you're being absurd. You know damn well that isn't true."

"How could I?" Sung turned his back, offended. "I have never seen this beast."

"You know what it is and why it is, and that's more than I know."

Sung turned again. "I made no such claim."

"It's why I'm here. You can't expect me to kill the beast until I know how it can be done. I can't fight it if I don't understand it—if its very existence doesn't make sense to me. You tell me everything you know about the beast and I'll go away and do your bidding."

"You lie," said Sung.

"I never lie," said Kaypack, with equal force.

"It's impossible—such knowledge cannot be shared."

"I have climbed Gorgan Mount—I know what resides there."

"It is not enough—you are not one of us."

"I still have to know."

"We cannot."

"Then," Kaypack said, "we'll stay here until you change your mind."

"That will not happen."

"Then the beast will not die." Their bitter eyes met and locked. Darcey sensed the battle raging between intractable wills. In the end, Sung looked away first. "You may accompany us to the village."

"All right," said Kaypack. "That'll be a start."

Shortly after they entered the forest and passed out of sight of the beach, a group of elders emerged silently from the trees and joined them. Darcey noted, dangling ahead, the sleek summit of Gorgan Mount, but the sight affected him only meagerly. Like everything else about Radius, the mountain seemed no more than a dimly recollected flash from something long forgotten. None of this intruded upon his life anymore. His ambition wasn't to climb the mountain; he wanted to slay the grayspace beast.

These new elders did not deign to speak, but Darcey guessed they were silently consulting with Sung. Kaypack also remained moodily quiet, as though he was mocking the elders. Darcey thought this was appropriate. After all, hadn't Kaypack climbed the mountain, too? In his own fashion, he was also an elder.

Nova whispered, "I'm scared." These were the first kind words she had spoken to Darcey since her anger in the ship's lounge. "It's so silent here—so awesome."

"I know. I'm scared, too." But that last part was a lie. Nothing about Radius frightened Darcey any longer.

At the village, they were met by the usual noisy throng of romping children. This familiar sight eased much of Nova's tension, and Darcey himself was struck with memories from his own boyhood. Scanning the faces of the children clustered nearby, Darcey sought to discover the familiar features of an old playmate or two. But these children were strangers; none seemed even vaguely known to him. A few of the elders he recalled from before, but not even many of them. It was as if, upon his departure, Radius had become a new and different world.

They were assigned to share a small hut between them. A young female child brought nuts, roots, leaves, and berries. Only Kaypack ate with a show of genuine eagerness. Nova, leaning against the wall of the hut, told Kaypack, "You haven't a chance, you know. These people—whatever they are—if they don't want to tell you something, they won't."

"Then I guess it's up to me to convince them they want to talk." He stuffed his mouth with a handful of ripe red berries.

"Good luck," Nova said, "but personally, I'm all on their side. If they know anything about the beast, they can keep it to themselves. Do you really want to go chasing after that thing?"

"Yes," Kaypack said, "I think I do."

"Now I know why they all say you're nuts."

When night came, Kaypack insisted that Nova and Darcey come with him into the central village. Here, the younger children played at booting a large shell back and forth between them. Darcey recognized the game and was again struck by an unwanted bolt of brief nostalgia. The surrounding forest glimmered with the flickering light reflected from the many campfires.

Kaypack chose to sit among the elders, and Darcey hesitantly joined him. After Nova also sat, Kaypack began to speak. "I fully understand that the death of the beast is important to you, but I also believe that it's not reasonable of you to expect me to act unless I know what I'm doing. You haven't seen the beast and I have. It's powerful—incredibly powerful—and for me to go chasing after it in total ignorance would be nothing less than suicide. I would fail—I'm not ashamed to tell you that—the beast would kill me, not me it." If the elders gathered in a circle around the fire heard a word Kaypack said, they gave no outward indication. Many closed their eyes. They appeared to be resting. "I'm a human being," Kaypack went on, "and your race is far older than mine. If you were capable of killing the beast yourselves, then I have to assume you'd do so—you wouldn't delegate the task to me. So because of that I've got to also assume that you respect my ability to take dramatic action. Somehow you believe that I'm more capable of killing than you are, and I also believe, because of that, that you're afraid of me."

Turning where he sat, Kaypack lifted a hand, indicating that Nova should stand. She looked angry, then hesitant, and then at last she stood.

Kaypack came to his feet, took Nova by the hand, and led her around the circle of elders. In front of each seated individual, Kaypack paused briefly. As he moved, he said, "This is Nova, a human being you've never met before. The reason I've brought her to you now is that Nova is much different from Darcey or me. She isn't exceptional. She's normal. I want you to understand what human beings are really like. I want you to bury the preconceptions you've formed from Darcey and me. Look at Nova, get to know her, understand her, then decide: Is she worthy of the knowledge I ask of you? If she isn't, then say so, refuse me. If she is, then tell me what I want to know. If Nova is worthy, then humanity is, too, and if that's so, then I believe the beast can be slain."

Kaypack completed two full circuits of the circle, then sat down. He drew a tobacco stick from some hidden nook of his silversuit and ignited the stub. Darcey had never seen Kaypack smoking before, but the gesture seemed appropriate to the moment.

Exhaling smoke, Kaypack said, "The decision is yours to make. I'm prepared to wait and hear what you say."

They remained within the circle all of that night, though no one ever spoke again. Even Nova remained awake and alert as the big fire gradually dwindled. By the time dawn's first light crept above the mountain peaks, only a smoldering pile of ashes remained to mark the location of the fire.

As if at a sign, the elders rose. One—not Sung—approached Kaypack. Standing nose to nose, the elder said, "We will inform you of our decision."

Kaypack nodded. "That's fair."

"We must know if you insist upon knowing everything or will accept a portion of the truth."

"All," said Kaypack.

"Then our answer must be yes or no."

"I'm agreed to that."

As the elders scattered, going either to their huts or to the adjoining fields, Kaypack stretched with an audible creak. "Well," he said, "that's over. Now let's get some sleep."

"Sleep?" Nova laughed. "Hell, I'm still scared. That was the weirdest experience of my life."

"You're not scared," said Kaypack, "you're impressed. There's a difference, Nova, and you ought to know it."

In their hut, as they lay curled in soft woven mats, Kaypack sleepily told Darcey, "I expect them to come to you with their answer, so be ready."

"Me?" Darcey opened his eyes. "Why me?"

"Because, as I told you before, you're one of them, closer to them than I'll ever be, Gorgan Mount or not. Just be ready."

In the days that followed, Kaypack frequently urged Darcey and Nova to spend as much time as possible away from the village. Having quickly grown bored with these too-familiar surroundings, Darcey eagerly took to showing Nova the nearby woods, the pond where he had once fished, and the great sea. Often in their wide wanderings they lost track of the hour and nightfall caught them in the open. When that occurred, they climbed a tree or found shelter in a bush and spent the night hidden there.

Two weeks may have passed—perhaps as many as three—when Sung came to Darcey to tell what the elders had decided.

Nova and Darcey sat beside a pool of green water and dipped their bare feet into the cooling shallows, when Sung appeared silently from the woods behind and sat between them without a word of greeting.

"Oh," Nova said, "you startled me."

Darcey realized there was no need to speak now; he was content to wait.

"I have come," Sung said, "to instruct you concerning the knowledge you seek."

"About the beast?" said Darcey.

"Yes."

"We're not Kaypack," Nova said. "He wants to know—not us."

"Kaypack said they might come to us instead of him," said Darcey.

"He meant you, not me."

Darcey could tell that Sung was waiting to say something more. He asked, "What is it?"

Sung said, "Before I can freely speak, you must first promise me that you will not divulge any of what I say to any other."

"Except Kaypack."

"Including Kaypack."

Darcey shook his head. "I'm afraid he'll never consent to that."

"He has."

"Kaypack?"

"He has stated that for us to tell you the information is sufficient. After you have heard, he will rely on your judgment."

"Oh," said Darcey, feeling the heavy weight of personal responsibility fall upon his shoulders. "Then I guess I agree—I promise."

"I'm going," said Nova, and she stood.

Sung touched her hand gently. "No, you must stay also. Kaypack was correct in calling you a proper human representative. For that reason, I must tell you both."

"And if I don't want to know?"

"Nova!" cried Darcey.

"You cannot be forced," said Sung.

"And I suppose you'll want me to promise, too. The same as Darcey—I'll keep my trap sealed."

"It is necessary."

Darcey realized that Nova, if she wished, could now destroy all of Kaypack's careful planning. She need only tell Sung no.

She said, "Yes," and sat down. "I can't help being curious," she told Darcey.

He could have kissed her—but didn't.

Sung shut his eyes. His body barely moving, his lips and chest frozen, he slid more deeply into a trance. Darcey felt himself drawn almost physically forward until the elder's serene silence became his own.

"In the beginning," Sung said, his voice approaching the regularity of a rhythmic chant, "we of Radius were much as you humans are now. We were many people then, not one, for each of us lived alone in isolation and knew nothing of those who lived beyond the meager range of our few senses. When one of us needed to speak, he could make use only of his lips, tongue, and throat. The soul was no more than a silent vessel that carried the spirit and served no other purpose until death came to claim the body. In time, we chose to extend the range of our senses. We saw farther, heard farther, and moved farther, but our souls remained dormant as before. Eventually, we roamed the stars and visited alien worlds and settled more than five hundred. Traveling the wastes of grayspace, we came to know that universe as well as our own.

"But, after the passage of some millennia, this outward quest lost interest for us, and we turned inward instead. It was then that our souls, so long quiescent, burst and blossomed and flowed freely. We came to realize that no one of us need ever be alone, and this discovery was sufficiently momentous that the stars themselves soon seemed insignificant. As we developed our souls more freely, we withdrew from the farther galactic boundaries and in time those of us who had survived once more dwelled strictly upon this planet, where our race had first reached conscious awareness. Here on Radius, we learned that our past endeavors had been futile, for the planet itself was not an accidental home but rather alive and aware, the conscious, living father of our race. We saw that its rivers were our blood, its soil our flesh, and its great seas and oceans our bodily organs. Radius, like each of us, possessed a soul, and we soon drew that forth and came to know it and sent it to dwell upon Gorgan Mount, where each of us could visit and learn the cosmic mysteries and therefore be free to be as one with the world that was our true father.

"Yet a soul is not whole—it is not merely one but also two. If there is good, there must also be matching evil. When our race was young, primitive priests spoke of the duality of existence. The universe was likened to a flat disc, with goodness occupying one side and evil the other. As science assumed control of our minds, we rejected this ancient concept and moved instead through an amoral landscape. In this we were wrong.

"So if goodness dwelled upon Gorgan Mount, so did evil, and the two soon fell into pitched combat. When this occurred, our personal souls, open and exposed, were torn and wounded. When evil emerged briefly dominant, wars raged across the surface of our globe, and millions perished in futile combat. When goodness prevailed, peace reigned, but there was seldom time to repair the old wounds before the terrible days came again. Our numbers dwindled drastically. A great fear seized our collective selves: in our new transcendental enlightenment, had we merely let loose the seeds that would end with our racial death?

"Therefore, in hopes of saving ourselves, we launched a new project designed to drive the forces of evil from their place upon Gorgan Mount. How this was accomplished I do not fully understand, but one day it was done. Evil left our world and fled to deep space. There, in exile, it waited, and so we dared not rest until the gates of the gray universe were driven open and the evil forces were lodged there forever."

"The grayspace beast," Darcey said.

"So I believe you know it."

"And we disturbed it? When we came?"

"And then," said Sung, chanting again, "a new and dominant race of human beings entered the gray domain, and the beast was disturbed. Within its evil soul, ancient longings stirred. At times, high upon Gorgan Mount, we feel vague hints of its desire to return. Not one thousand years ago, an elder committed an act of senseless murder. Soon afterward another man stripped away his own life. Once two children built personal weapons. Its tendrils have reached us. Can the beast itself lie far behind?"

"But it's in grayspace," Darcey said. "I know—I saw it there."

"For the human race," said Sung, "the situation is much different. Good and evil reside within you, caught in the cosmic balance. You can control your beast—we cannot."

"But can't you," said Darcey, "drive the beast away as you did before? Since you defeated it once, why be afraid of it now?"

"Alas," said Sung, "we have lost that power. Too many aeons have passed. We no longer know the secrets of our ancestors. Other alternatives have been considered. Some have suggested waging war against humanity and thus preventing you from contaminating the beast with your presence. But we are too weak. We have lost the strain of evil necessary to fight a winning war. No, your race is our only hope. We are wise enough—but only you are strong enough."

"Then how?" Nova spoke for the first time.

"I don't—" Sung began.

"How are we supposed to do this little job for you? I've been sitting here the last hour listening to your mumbo-jumbo about souls and evil spirits and all the rest and I've been waiting patiently for you to get around to answering Kaypack's question. We came here to find out how to kill the beast. We don't give a damn what it is or who. We've got to know how."

"There may be many possible ways," Sung said.

"Then name me one," said Nova.

"I—I can't," said Sung, unable to evade her attack again.

"Thanks," said Nova, with a smirk, "that's all I wanted to know."

"But there may be many ways," said Sung, pleading. "You are the strong ones, not us. You must find these paths."

"And if somehow we don't? If somehow we aren't quite as strong as you give us credit for? Then what?"

Sung shook his head sadly. "The decision is yours to make." He faced Darcey. "Do you have any questions you wish to ask of me?"

Darcey shook his head. "No, I don't think so. Except—is it all right to tell Kaypack what you've told us? That we know now what the beast is and how it was created?"

"You may tell him that but you must not repeat any of the history."

"And is it all right if I tell him how crazy this is, how you haven't helped us at all?" Nova said.

"You may state your opinion."

"It's only the facts that support the opinion I have to keep quiet about."

"You have promised."

"Isn't that rather like eating the pea before the shells are maneuvered?"

Sung, confused, shook his head. "I don't understand."

"I said it wasn't fair."

"Is the extinction of our race fair?" asked Sung.

"That," Nova said, "depends on who you're asking. Do you want my opinion, your opinion, or the beast's opinion?"

"To survive," Sung said, "we are willing to risk everything else."

"I'll tell Kaypack you said that," Nova said.

When she and Darcey met with Kaypack in the village and told him what little they could, he gave no immediate response. "I guess that does it," he said.

The finality of this surprised Darcey. "But you came here to find out about the beast and you still don't know any more now than when you came."

"But you two know."

"We can't tell you anything."

"But you can act on the knowledge you possess—that's got to be enough for me."

Darcey couldn't understand why this should be so. "But you're the commander. You have the responsibility."

"Darcey," Kaypack said briskly, "let's pack."

Two elders—neither one was Sung—appeared to guide them through the forest. Their shuttle remained as they'd left it upon the sandy beach.

Kaypack used the communicator to call the *Arjuna*, orbiting above. Welch's round face appeared in the viewscreen. "You're finished?" said his voice.

"I'm coming back."

"We'll be waiting," said Welch, with a broad, open smile.

"You've got to be kidding," said a student.

It was time to assume my ingénue identity again. "About what?"

"Who puts those words into Sung's mouth? Souls, spirits, living planets. Nobody's considered that guff in centuries. It's not only stupid, it's been disproved."

"Maybe the Radians didn't know that. They didn't have you around to tell them."

"If they were so damn superior, they had to know."

"And if they weren't," I prodded.

"Huh?"

"Maybe," I said softly, "they aren't as superior as they want you—or Darcey—to think."

"Which means?"

I refused to be baited. "You tell me."

"Now about the beast," said another, "you can't expect to get away with that explanation, can you? Good and evil are abstract, relative concepts, quite meaningless in any—"

"Don't lecture me." That was pride speaking. "I think I already know that much."

"You don't seem to think we do."

"No, no." I saw that I was going to have to lead their little noses more directly than I might have wished. "Quit confusing your aesthetic responses with the story itself. I wasn't the one who described the beast—not directly I wasn't—it was Sung. If you have any argument, it's with him."

I was thankful to discover I'd said enough. "In other words," one of my most backward students said, "Sung told a lie."

"He didn't tell the truth."

"There's a difference?"

I nodded. "That's for you to decide."

After the shuttle's return from the Radian surface, Kaypack refused to wait an unnecessary moment. He gathered the entire crew around him in the ship's lounge and then asked Darcey and Nova to explain what they had learned from Sung and why they were not permitted to reveal any of it openly.

Welch's frown seemed almost gleeful. "Then what you're saying, Kaypack, is that you know nothing more now than you did before."

"That's true—I don't. Darcey and Nova do."

"And they can't tell us anything?"

"They can only act upon the knowledge they do possess."

"I think we ought to vote on that," Welch said.

Kaypack agreed. "I have nothing more to add." He then asked everyone present to state an opinion in turn.

Welch voted first: "We go after the money."

Maria said, "I think I've been getting loony lately because I've half hoped you'd come up with something, Kaypack. You haven't. It's duller this way, but I'm with Rickard."

Johann said, "This foolishness has proceeded far enough. We all came here to perform specific tasks. This beast nonsense is only an unnecessary waste of time. I believe Mr. Welch is absolutely correct. We must get back to business."

Darcey and Kaypack were not eligible to vote.

Veador hung his head. "My loyalty to my commander must take precedence over my good judgment. I support his position."

The Simerians, in lilting unison, said, "Chase the beast."

That left only Nova. Darcey turned with the others to

gaze at her. The smugness of the smile on her lips puzzled and surprised him. She said, "What the hell, I think I'll vote to chase the beast."

Welch turned on her with blazing anger. "You young idiot —they've brainwashed you!"

Nova grinned. "Maybe so, but a vote's a vote. Did you really expect someone like me—dumb and ignorant all her life —not to want to play with the first real secret she's ever had?"

"You poor fool!" said Welch.

Nova glowered. "Say that again and I'll pop you in the gut."

Welch backed off, still glaring.

Kaypack announced, "I'm going below to repair that broken engine. Veador, I'll want your help."

"Yes, my commander."

But before Kaypack could get away, Welch first insisted that the vote was unfair; the Simerians, he asserted, should have been allowed only one vote between them. When Kaypack refused to accept this, even Maria agreed. "Don't be such an ass, Rickard. You can't change the rules after the game's been played."

Welch remained unconvinced. "Kaypack," he said, "if you get us killed, I swear I'll have your head."

Within a common-day's time, the *Arjuna* had moved free of Radian orbit and begun its long drive toward the farther reaches of outer space, where the gray universe could be easily reached and invaded.

The final search had commenced.

"Hooray for Nova!" said my students.

I smiled. "Then you agree with her?"

"Hell, no, she's out of her head. But it sure makes the story a lot more interesting this way."

I had to agree with that.

FIVE

My students sat like robots in rows, arms folded, eyes fixed. "What?" I had to say. "Don't tell me nobody has anything to say."

"We're waiting."

I casually scratched myself. "Really? What for?"

"To be shown."

"Shown what?" I could see this was intended seriously.

"To be shown that you haven't been completely wasting our time these past few hours."

"Oh." Struck damn near dumb. "Oh, I see."

Ah, pressure, tension, pressure. The burdens a teacher must bear.

The day before the *Arjuna* was scheduled to make its leap into the gray wilderness, Darcey, recently relieved of watch, wandered purposively forward through the ship's straight, slender corridors till he reached a certain passageway. Here, kneeling, he watched Nova's twisting tail as she squatted slightly ahead, straining her elbow with a bristly brush and a bucket of hot water.

"Okay, I admit I was stupid," she confessed past a shoulder. "I mean, here I was thinking like an idiot that just because I'd saved Kaypack's stupid rear for him with my crazy vote, he might actually want to express a certain amount of gratitude. Was I really so naïve? A promotion—a chance to get off my knees and do some intelligent work. Why not

Welch? I asked him. Our alien specialist. Why not let me do that and him this?" She showed Darcey the wire brush, a handy symbol of the job at hand. "I could train him. I could tell him what to clean and what to scrub, what to polish and what to wash. So what does Kaypack say?" She resumed her work, building a stream of bright soap bubbles. "He tells me that every crew position is already snugly filled by the person best qualified for handling the work. He actually said that. So you tell me, Darcey, since he's your pal: How does my peculiar breeding and education especially equip me for being a scrub serf?"

Darcey glanced at the bright deck exposed beneath Nova's knees. "You've got to admit you're doing a beautiful job."

"So what? I'm a perfectionist. I'd do a beautiful job as an alien specialist, too."

"But Welch isn't."

"Huh?"

"He'd do a lousy job on the decks. Obviously, Kaypack feels you're irreplaceable."

"Oh, go fly up," she told him, scrubbing and straining again.

But this was not the purpose for which Darcey had sought out Nova. Because they had both been kept busy since their return from Radius, not until now had time appeared for asking the most pertinent question of all. "Nova, how come you voted the way you did?"

She didn't look back. "Because it was the way I felt at the time."

"On Radius you seemed to feel completely the opposite."

"Then you misinterpreted me. I hadn't made up my mind."

"When did you?"

"How can I answer that? Sometime before the vote was taken—you can't expect me to give you the exact minute."

"But you should be able to tell me why."

Laying her brush aside and nudging the bucket so that it

didn't block her way, Nova turned. "You are insistent, aren't you?"

"I like to know why people do things."

"Well, I can tell you why it wasn't; it wasn't because of the Radians and their terrible plight."

"You weren't concerned for them?"

"Nope." Her eyes studied the corridor fore and aft; plainly, she did not wish to be overheard. "I can't be concerned with arrogance. Who did they have to blame for the mess except themselves? Who the hell did they think they were? Driving evil out of their souls. I thought that was the most pompous trick I'd ever heard of. Who wants to be totally good? You maybe, but not me. Evil is too much fun."

"Like Welch and Maria," he said.

"Maria maybe—she's starting to come around—but not Welch. He's no more evil than a bucket of hot water. He's ignorant, shortsighed, half blind. I'll tell you which of us is the most evil: your old buddy Kail Kaypack, that's who."

"Oh, don't be funny." She was baiting him. Yet, where was that glint that usually filled her eyes?

"Then how come the elders selected him?" she asked. "Why not you or me or Johann Helsing?"

"Because they knew Commander Kaypack. He'd lived among them and climbed Gorgan Mount. They knew he was strong and forceful and courageous and good."

"He may be all those things, but if he is, it's because he's evil first. The thing with Kaypack—Kaypack since he's come out here, because he wasn't the same person on Paradise Planet—is that he's learned to channel his worst drives and put them to the best purposes. Evil works for Kaypack, not against him."

Darcey shook his head. "I still don't understand."

"Then take me, for instance. What kind of person am I? Good? Sure, sometimes, maybe. Evil? Most of the time. How come? Because, basically, I'm curious. I remember when I lived on a planet where there were fighting contests. The fighters—supposedly men—were more metal and plastic than flesh or bone. They stood toe to toe in the middle of a roped-off arena till one or the other managed to pound the other to death with his fists. Huge crowds came to cheer. Part of the fun was to choose a favorite—there was little betting—and yell for that guy to win. How come? Bloodlust? That's part of it. But curiosity, too. Which guy was tougher? I went myself because I wanted to know, and if my favorite didn't win, at least I knew he wasn't good enough."

"I think I understand, but—"

"Kaypack or the beast. That's what I'm saying. I want to know which is tougher."

Darcey was incredulous. "And that's the only reason you voted to go?"

"Not the only one, no, but a pretty good one, I think."

He wasn't sure whether he ought to try to believe her. Either she was half crazy or half brilliant. But which? "You may get killed yourself finding out."

She grinned. "That's the risk." Turning and bending, she dipped the edge of her brush into the bubbly water.

Darcey edged forward. "But which one are you rooting for?"

She shook her head. "Can't you tell? Kaypack, of course. I'm not crazy, you know."

He sighed, satisfied, and backed off. "I hope you're right."

She spun with an eager smile and thrust out a hand. "Then bet me. That way, even if I win, we can celebrate together."

"There'll be no betting here," I thought I ought to warn them before proceeding. "It's strictly forbidden in the rules."

I got laughed at for my bother. "So who wants to bet?" said a student. "It's pretty damn obvious, isn't it?"

I shook my head. "No, I don't think so."

Hoo-haw, as they laughed again. "We think you ought to pay more attention to your own story," they said.

"I do," I protested.

They let me off with wide grins this time. "Want to bet on that, pops?"

I refused politely and, improvising quickly, came up with: "How about some last cameos?"

They seemed well enough agreed, which put me in a sudden bind.

I coped divinely.

Alone with Welch in a dim, bolted, seldom-used storage closet, Maria told him frankly, "He beat our asses off."

From Welch's steady, enraged expression, Maria inferred that she had said the wrong thing. His voice, when it came at last, reeked with bitterness and something more: "How can you accept this situation as final? One idiot girl. It's her fault we're here at all. If not for her, I'd be in command of this cruiser and we'd all be rich."

"So soon?" Maria wanted to be fair. "I only said it's too late to do anything about it."

"But we can't give up," said Welch, drawing so close that his face nearly touched hers. "That thing—that beast—may kill us all."

"Not if I can help it," Maria said. She edged gradually back from him.

"Good." He paused to huff. "Since we're agreed, the next step is to do something."

"But we're not agreed." She tried a smile, but the light wasn't sufficiently bright to show it.

He grew excited instantly. "Damn it, you said—"

"I said I wasn't going to let the beast kill me. I meant just that: not without a fight."

"You'll co-operate with them?" He seemed amazed.

She tried frankness again. "Yes."

He huffed monstrously this time, and his cheeks in the faint light seemed to bloat. "You're deserting me. Damn it, this is treachery."

"I call it realism. Damn it, Rickard, haven't you noticed the difference out here? On Paradise Planet it was fine. Money was everything, so why not share the common obsession? But out here? What can money mean? My God, come down to the control room and look at the stars. Remember grayspace? Remember how beautiful Radius looked hanging in the void like a jewel in a dark cup? This isn't new. I've been thinking this way more and more. I just don't care if I get rich or not."

"You're soft," he said coldly.

"But at least I'm not afraid."

He leaned forward, glowering, and made as if to grab her. "What do you mean by that?"

"You're afraid of the beast."

"Damn liar."

"You haven't even seen it and yet it scares you to death." She saw no further reason to be kind. "A man like you—anything you can't directly control is frightening. No wonder you treated poor Kaypack like a joke. But look who's laughing now."

"I'll break you, Maria. You're ruined from this moment on."

Deliberately, she laughed in his face. "You poor simple bastard. You can't do anything to harm me out here."

"I'll see you dead."

Maria had already started toward the door, but now she hesitated. With one hand on the lock, smiling tightly, she said, "If I die, you won't be there to see it, because you'll be just as dead as I am, Welch. The beast won't play any favorites. Your position won't help you then. No wonder you're scared. The beast will kill you dead."

Welch did not reply.

Standing watch with the silent Simerians, Johann Helsing stood close to the glittering control panel and studied the pile of navigational star charts that lay there.

This work wasn't necessary. The *Arjuna* was on its way

toward grayspace. Until the jump, no new charts were needed. What Helsing was actually doing now—he would not have wished to admit this to anyone—was having fun.

The game went this way: Helsing selected a star at random —one anywhere within the charted galaxy—and then attempted to plot the best possible course (ignoring the existence of grayspace) from here to there. Sometimes, for no reason except to increase the fun, he purposely charted the ship's course so that it intersected a binary or a black hole or some other complex gravitational force.

Why was he so intent on having fun? All his life, neither an especially long nor short one, he had never deliberately played a game before. So why now?

Helsing wasn't entirely sure of the answer to that, but he did think it had something to do with a strange, unique (to him) feeling that had recently visited him, a perception, a belief, that some sort of final ending was about to occur. Was this his own death? He wasn't sure of that, either, but he did know that he firmly believed that if he failed to do this now, didn't play games or have fun, if he didn't spend every possible waking moment in that abstract mathematical realm that was his chosen home, then he might never get another chance again.

This ending—he did not fear it. What, after all, was even death except the brisk motion of a soft eraser wiping clean a dirty slate? If anything, Helsing anticipated the impending moment—he was eager for a chance to change.

But he was also in a hurry to finish and be done with this old life before the new one (even if it proved merely to be death) at last arrived.

As Helsing scribbled, a portion of the control panel buried beneath his piled charts began to flicker. Finally noticing the light, Helsing thrust his papers aside and hastily turned the proper knob. In the rear viewscreen, Commander Kaypack appeared. He sat comfortably in his stateroom.

"Where were you?" asked Kaypack's voice.

"Right here, sir. All the time." He removed his spectacles and cleaned them rapidly, a trace of the old nerves. "Ask them, if you don't believe me."

He meant the cooing, cuddling Simerians.

"I don't think that's necessary," said Kaypack, "but, tell me, what's up?"

"Oh, nothing, sir." He replaced his shiny spectacles. "Just some calculations."

Kaypack shook his head, surprised. "You told me sixteen hours—that hasn't changed?"

"Oh, no, sir, this was something else."

"Well, what? It's not a secret, is it?"

"No, of course not. But it is"—he searched his brain for the correct word, "it's private."

"But that isn't why I called you. I want to hold a brief general meeting of the crew in the ship's lounge. I'd like you to call everybody for me."

Helsing glanced at his charts. "Will that be soon, sir?"

"As soon as everyone's been called."

"Me, too?"

"You're a crew member, aren't you?"

Bleakly: "Yes, sir."

"Then that should answer your question."

After the screen went blank, Helsing turned again to the crowded pile of papers. Lifting the ones on which he had made his scribbled calculations, he turned the pages slowly, studying the symbols, graphs, figures, and diagrams that filled each separate sheet. As surely as he had sensed that an ending was coming, he was now convinced that the time for play was over.

These were sheets of paper. Papers with pointless things written upon them. These belonged not to this world but to that other one—that old one.

Helsing took the papers one by one and tore each neatly into four quarters.

He allowed the torn sheets to flutter uselessly to the floor. When he finished, he began to call the crew.

Before Veador entered the ship's lounge to attend his commander's scheduled meeting, he first paused in the doorway long enough to confirm that everyone else (except the commander) was already present in the room.

Tucking his tail carefully underneath, he seated himself in a chair set safely aside from the others.

Moving his gaze surreptitiously around the room, Veador cautiously studied the waiting faces. There was very little talk, and he noted nothing that might present a danger to his commander. Nova sat perched upon the edge of a chair and her expression radiated eager interest. Maria Novitsky, more relaxed, crossed her feet languidly and gazed at the distant ceiling. Helsing, too, seemed more serene and detached than usual; he chatted quietly with Darcey, who sat eagerly coiled beside him. Poor Rickard Welch occupied a position as willingly lonely as Veador's own. Crouched upon the floor near the front of the room, he appeared pale and drawn, silent and obviously in pain. The Simerians were also present; as always, Veador strained to ignore them.

With a slim sheaf of papers clutched tightly in one hand, Kail Kaypack entered the lounge with abrupt haste. Reaching his place at the front of the room, he turned at once but did not smile.

"My fellow stellars," he said, "the reason I've asked to speak to you now, only mere hours before our impending jump into grayspace, is because I believe we have certain important and necessary business to transact. To begin, I've established a revised duty roster and want to be sure everyone understands his or her assignment." Kaypack read from the top sheet of paper. "After we jump, Darcey and Nova will stand an eight-hour watch. Maria and Johann will follow them, while the third and final watch will be stood by Rickard and myself. I further want Johann to prepare a detailed navigation chart that will permit the *Arjuna* to make a leisurely circuit through grayspace without ever losing track of its general location. We're setting out to search for the beast, so I want to give it every possible chance of finding us. The Simerians will assist Veador in the engine room. The three of them can work out their own schedule, but I want to take every possible measure toward preventing a recurrence of the malfunction that stymied us the last time we pursued the beast. To assist in this, I intend to spend as much time as possible myself in the control room during other watches. Any sightings of the beast, confirmed or not, should be reported immediately to me." He glanced up at last from the paper and his eyes briefly scanned the room. "And only me."

Welch, in sudden agitation, lifted an arm and shook the fingers frantically. "But then what?" he cried.

"Then what what?" asked Kaypack, still not smiling.

"Then what do we do? Assuming we sight this so-called beast. Do we chase it again?"

Kaypack shook his head. "No, we attack."

"Would you mind—?"

"In a moment." Kaypack looked deliberately away from Welch. "The rest of you? Any questions?"

There were none.

Kaypack turned the papers he held, exposing a second sheet. "This is something I want to read to you. It's my—" He halted, suddenly flustered. "My will." He cleared his throat and went on, stronger than before. "My last will and testament."

A sharp, horrified intake of breath hissed through the room.

Kaypack shook his head shyly. "I appreciate your concern, but this is—I'm afraid—it is necessary." He fastened his eyes to the paper he held and spoke in a clear, unemotional voice. He might have been reciting a newly revised duty roster. "The reason I bring this up now, and publicly, is also to answer Rickard's last question. In view of our lack of unanimity concerning the beast, I just can't feel it would be fair for me to expose the rest of you to any unnecessary danger. For that reason, in the event we do sight and catch the beast, I intend to conduct the final assault alone in a shuttle. For that reason—" He held up a hand, silencing both Nova and Darcey, who had popped to their feet. "For that reason, I feel this document is now necessary."

Kaypack began to read, his tone even more lifeless than before. "I, Kail Kaypack, commander of the grayspace cruiser *Arjuna*, a man of established intelligence and rationality, do hereby establish the following provisions in the event of my death. One, that all those items of personal property belonging to me or currently held in my possession should be divided according to choice among the present members of my crew. In the event of an irreconcilable division arising over the ownership of a particular item, then that item shall immediately revert to the care of my loyal assistant and good friend, the engineer Veador, who has during many decades of service never sought any form of reward from me."

In spite of the sadness of the occasion, Veador felt a warm, tingling sensation glowing in the tips of his hands and feet. He came near to smiling in real delight; his commander did love him, after all.

"Two," said Kaypack, continuing, "title to the cruiser *Arjuna* shall be returned to Darcey in hopes that he will find a noble and reasonable use for the ship. I make no stipulations whatsoever concerning its future use. The cruiser will belong to Darcey, and Darcey alone."

"I'll use it to hunt the beast, sir," Darcey cried, but Kaypack did not appear to hear.

"Three," he said, "any stray currency in my possession, the remnants of the sum advanced to me by Darcey, shall be returned to him. I would hope that he will see fit to share this amount, meager as it is, with his fellow stellars. Four, my notebooks, occasional scribblings, snippets of autobiography, and poems shall be immediately destroyed upon my death.

To ensure that this request is carried out, I would like to stipulate that the two Simerian members of my crew carry out this task. I am well aware not only of their loyalty but also of their unconcern for more than transitory matter. Five," said Kaypack, looking up now as though this passage stood clear in his mind, "I just want to express a portion of the gratitude I feel to those of you who have served with me in this my last crew. Without your help, I could never have written this will, for until you came into my life, I owned nothing worth leaving to another generation."

Smiling suddenly, Kaypack dropped his hands. The papers clutched in his fist brushed the crease of his silversuit. "Any questions, then—or objections?"

Only Welch had anything to say. "You know you may not die," he said, turning the words into a near accusation.

Kaypack shook his head. "That's a possibility, I admit."

As he watched Kaypack turn to leave the lounge, Veador understood that his commander had finally succeeded in accomplishing the most difficult task of all.

Kail Kaypack had firmly established himself as commander of the *Arjuna* and its crew.

It had taken his death to do that.

"My, my," said a boy in the first row, wiping a mock tear from his eye, "that's really the saddest thing I've ever heard." Then he giggled.

I admit I bridled and, happily, so did some of the more sensitive, advanced students. Speaking first, with considerable restraint, I said, "We're talking about a man's life here. It may not be sad, but it is—or should be—serious."

"Sure," the boy agreed. "Except when it's so much bullcrap." Again, the giggling. "Like that last will and testament."

Not for the first time since my decision to stay and teach, I considered the possibility that these children belonged to a new and mutant species.

As if to confirm my fear, the first boy suddenly developed a supporter. "There was really no need for any of that soapy stuff," said a girl. "In my opinion, Welch was correct. Even if Kaypack died, who would fight over the junk he left behind? And why do it publicly like that? He could have tucked his last will away in some obvious nook and waited for somebody to discover and read it after he was dead."

"But that's just the point, stupid." This wasn't me but one of my brighter boys. "The last three sentences are the real keys. Kaypack didn't read the will because he cared what happened after he was dead. He did it to show them how serious he was. He did it to solidify his support, to reach them on a strictly emotional level. He was being calculating—sly. Can't any of you see that?"

I was amazed to discover a general nodding of heads throughout the little room.

I'll tell you what it did: it made me feel (briefly) like a damn fool sentimentalist.

I recovered rapidly. "That's exactly the way it was," I told them.

After all, who says an author has any better insight than another person into the real meaning of his work?

The first sighting of the beast (Darcey learned later) occurred only a few short hours after jump.

It was Rickard Welch who did the spotting.

He stood watch with Kaypack. No one else was present in the control room at the moment of the sighting. Welch stared open-mouthed and trembling at the speck of moving silver that glimmered in the lower right corner of the rear viewscreen. "It's here," he said softly. "Damn it, I can see it myself."

Kaypack looked up from where he was sitting. "What can you see, Rickard?"

"The beast," Welch said, still staring.

"What?" said Kaypack, cupping his nearest ear. "I didn't quite catch—"

"The beast!" shouted Welch, turning in a sudden rage. "It's here to kill us."

When Welch turned to shout at Kaypack, he also blinked (for the first time since the sighting).

Kaypack padded over to see. He peered at the viewscreen, blinked, and peered more deeply. "I'm afraid I can't make out anything like that, Rickard." Kaypack shrugged apologetically, backing off from the screen. "Maybe it's these old eyes of mine."

"Damn it," said Welch, in a rage, "you know as well as I do it's gone now." This was true. Welch stared and peered and stared, but the silver speck had vanished.

Kaypack spoke kindly. "Rickard, are you sure it—?"

"Yes, you damn old fool. Do I look like someone who sees things?"

"No, of course not." Kaypack smiled reassuringly and actually patted Welch's shoulder. "I apologize, Rickard. I believe you saw the beast."

"Don't patronize me, goddamn it!" Welch jerked away.

An abrupt change came over Kaypack's features, and when he spoke again his voice was not only serious but sincere. "That was the beast."

Welch looked surprised. His voice betrayed a sudden uncertainty. "It was?"

Kaypack again patted his shoulder. "You damn bet it was."

Darcey, when he heard this story from Nova, who had heard it from Maria, who had heard it from Welch himself, laughed. "I bet," he said, "that was just Kaypack's way of making sure Welch was one of us. Now that he's seen the beast with his own eyes, he won't get around it by saying 'mythical beast' anymore."

But Nova frowned. "I'm not so sure, Darcey."

"Sure about what?"

"Well, when Maria told me about the story, she said that Welch, when he told her, was shaking he was so scared. Sometimes I think he believes in the beast more than any of us. That's why he's so scared. He knows it's real and he knows what it can do."

"How could he?"

"You'd have to ask him," said Nova.

The *Arjuna* traveled through grayspace for a total of forty-four common days. Darcey reckoned the voyage in terms of eleven-day periods. During the first, the excitement and enthusiasm generated by Kaypack's reading of his will remained at a fever pitch. Everyone in the crew sought the beast. False sightings (excluding Welch's) were rampant. When he dreamed, Darcey himself seldom envisioned anything but the vast gray specter. It was eleven days of eager oneness. The crew wanted to find the beast and kill it; they thought of nothing else.

The second eleven-day period resembled the first at least superficially, but Darcey noticed one phenomenon in particular: during the first period, everyone thought, dreamed, ate, and slept the beast; during the second, everyone merely talked. When not standing watch, the crew gathered in their quarters and competed to see who could most loudly proclaim his or her desire to see the beast dead. Only Welch stayed apart from this. Welch continued to do battle with an ambiguous demon of his own devising.

During the third period of eleven days, the talk abruptly ceased. Darcey went days without ever hearing the beast mentioned. People stood their assigned watches, gulped down the concentrated food prepared by Nova, and slept. During one watch, Nova fell fast asleep in the control room. When Darcey angrily shook her awake, she denied having been asleep. "I thought I saw the beast," she said. "You know you have to blink when that happens."

"You don't blink by keeping your eyes shut for five minutes," he said.

"Maybe you don't—I do." She tried to smile but managed nothing more than a yawn.

Darcey decided that if the first period was dominated by excitement and the second by talk, then the key word for the third was boredom.

During the fourth period, that boredom changed to irritation, then open anger. People discussed the beast again. They said that it did not exist.

"But, damn it," said Darcey, pointing an angry finger at Helsing, "you saw it yourself. You know that. With your own goddamn eyes."

"Maybe I did and maybe I didn't," Helsing said primly. "After all, one's senses are limited instruments. Even the eyes have been known to lie."

"And my eyes? And Kaypack's eyes? And the Radians' eyes? What's wrong with you people? Have you all gone crazy?"

From his nook in the corner, Welch laughed. "No, but I think maybe someone else has."

Only Nova's quick intervention prevented an actual fistfight.

On the fortieth day, Darcey did get involved in a fight with Welch. He lost—but his heart wasn't involved.

On the forty-fourth day, Nova announced, "We're running out of food."

Darcey looked up from his bunk. The crew sat languidly around their quarters. Only Welch, who stood watch with Kaypack, was absent. "Have you told the commander?" asked Darcey.

"I've been trying for a week. He won't listen."

"And so we starve to death," said Maria, her anger mounting already.

"The man is becoming obsessed," said Helsing.

"He's going to have to do it on an empty stomach pretty soon," said Nova.

Darcey sighed. With a fifth eleven-day period about to begin, he knew action could no longer be delayed. "I think I ought to go talk to him," he said. "After his watch."

"I think somebody better," Maria said, and there was more than a hint of a threat in her tone. "I came along because the rest of you convinced me it was right. Now I'm beginning to wonder. Does Kaypack intend to stay in this gray mess forever? I don't know about the rest of you, but this isn't where I want to die."

"It isn't where Kaypack wants to die, either," Darcey said, "but he's willing to do it."

"Oh, bullcrap," said Maria. Helsing nodded his agreement. Nova merely smiled—and only slightly.

"I said I'd talk to him," said Darcey bleakly.

Kaypack answered Darcey's fourth knock. From inside his stateroom, he called out that it was all right for Darcey to come in. When he entered, Darcey discovered Kaypack reclining upon a hard cot. A wet cloth lay draped across his eyes. Kaypack, it appeared, was also growing weary from the ordeal of waiting.

"Sir," Darcey said politely, searching for a chair, "the crew asked me to come here and talk to you. Nova says our food stores are getting dangerously low."

"I think she may have mentioned that to me, too." Kaypack's voice sounded muffled even though the wet cloth covered only the top quarter of his face.

"She says if we don't jump to normal space soon, we'll run the risk of starving."

Kaypack's whole body moved as he shrugged. "The beast doesn't know that."

"I don't think the crew cares about the beast anymore, sir."

Kaypack smiled like a fellow conspirator. "But we do, don't we, Darcey?"

"I don't want to starve, sir."

Kaypack suddenly sat up. He tossed aside the wet cloth, and, when he saw his eyes, Darcey couldn't restrain a smile of relief. Kaypack hadn't changed. The old flame of eagerness burned as brightly as ever. "Then what do you suggest we do?"

Darcey felt his brain operating at a dizzy pace. Until he spoke, he had no idea what his mind wanted him to say. "I think we should act like we're going home, sir."

Kaypack did not seem disturbed by this. In fact, he nodded. "But why?"

"Because what we've done so far just hasn't worked. The beast is out there, as we both know, sir. I can feel it—can't you? It's lurking somewhere near us, but it won't come close."

"Do you think it may be frightened?"

Darcey had never considered this possibility. Could the beast be that human? Did it act from motivations, the way a man might? "I wouldn't know, sir, but I doubt it. After all, there's no good reason why it should be."

"You mean, there's no reason we know of."

"Yes, sir."

"But you still think we should run for it."

"To lure the beast, sir. The crew is impatient, getting afraid again. If we start to run, they'll calm down. Even if the beast doesn't come, we can still jump, obtain additional provisions, then come back."

Kaypack looked suddenly weary. "No, we can't."

"But—"

Kaypack came alive, fists clenched, full of passion, a taut vein showing on his forehead. "I've composed everything toward this moment. It's like a symphony, Darcey, and you can't delay the crescendo too long. If we ever leave, the crew will quit. I can't blame them. They'll have time to think."

"Then it's now or never."

Kaypack nodded.

"But still think . . ." His mind suddenly stopped. What did he think?

"Yes, Darcey?"

Abruptly, the answer came to him. "I think we better do it."

Kaypack sighed. "I know."

I paused briefly here in order to inform them, "The story's nearly finished now, so I want you to keep your collective traps shut and let me get it done with."

"What about the questions?" said one.

I should have known better than to expect to get off so easily. "What questions?"

"The ones you've never bothered to answer. Like about yourself. If you won't deny that you're either Darcey or Kaypack, then what exactly is your relationship to this story?"

I grinned. "Whatever it is, it has nothing to do with the story itself. Let me finish that first."

They were pouting. "Well, that's hardly all you haven't told us."

I decided it was time to be sympathetic. "I see what you mean, but I don't think it would be fair or sensible or especially artistic if I now went back over the whole story to fill in the holes you claim are there. Besides, you were the ones who demanded subtlety. Use your heads, study the characters, and I think most everything will become clear."

"Except the characters," came a stinger.

I winced. "But I've told you—"

"Sure," said my scorpion avatar (actually, a tiny blonde with top-heavy breasts), "you started out that way, but for hours and hours it's been Darcey, Darcey, Darcey. How are we supposed to know what Welch is thinking? How come he's so scared of the beast? What about these mysterious

Simerians? I'm not saying you haven't been subtle, I'm just saying you haven't told us everything we ought to know."

Stung to the quick—her idea, I'm sure—I bit my lip. "Okay," I finally said. "There's time"—they groaned—"to pause a few minutes. Let's take the crew one by one and see how they're thinking. But not before. No backtracking. How they're thinking right now. Is that okay?"

I got several yawns—from the class dummies, largely—but no objections.

I tried not to wipe the tension-sweat from my forehead. Keep cool, keep cool. What the hell? I asked myself. How many times have you pulled this off before, and you're still scared?

Well, I was.

Or had been.

The hump had been breached.

The narrator (that's me) plunged on.

Unstately, plump Rickard Welch crept into the secluded storeroom, shut the door with a whisper, and dimmed the light above.

Goddamn, he thought, can they really be serious about giving up?

The half-alien kid (Darcey) had arrived with the news. As soon as he'd bustled into the crew quarters wearing an unexpected grin, Welch had grown instantly suspicious. His body tightened, his mouth ran dry, his fists clenched. Something stunk. Something was happening that should not.

Darcey said, "I've just spoken with Commander Kaypack and he agrees with us. He's already gone up to the control room to change the ship's course and he wants you, Johann, to chart a new course that'll allow us to make our jump close to an inhabited world."

"Why?" said Welch, barely able to control his shaking voice.

Darcey shrugged. "I guess because he doesn't want to starve any more than we do."

Welch had realized at once that that was a lie. Starving. Kaypack would never have feared something as banal as that.

Therefore, his action was not only unexpected, it was also inexplicable, and that was much, much worse.

So Welch had quickly come here.

It was the same as the beast. Welch knew that the others—even Maria now—felt he was nothing more than greedy. The beast interfered with his desire for planetary exploitation and thus Welch opposed the hunt. He did not deny the presence of a certain element of truth in this charge, but the fools failed to go beyond their single platitude. Sure, he wanted to be rich. He never had been and the desire ran so great within him that he could taste it on his tongue most times.

But why? They never asked that. Why was wealth so important to Rickard Welch?

Again, it was the same as the beast.

He had been born a backworlder. A planet only tentatively explored but apparently beautiful. A real paradise, not a sharpie's joke like the gambling world. Trees. Vegetation. Lakes, rivers, white mountains. A clean, crisp wind that never blew too hard. Wildlife. Room to roam.

The planet had been partially settled a dozen years before Welch's birth by the religious sect to which his parents belonged: the Predestinists, who believed that every universal action was part of an immense cycle and that all things had happened many hundreds of times before. They also believed in a benevolent God.

Born among these people, Welch also believed. At eighteen common years, he left his homeworld for the first time and scanned with two friends to a nearby world in order to see the sights. When he returned, he discovered that the entire Predestinist settlement had, during his absence, become a massive crater filled with hot ash.

There were no survivors.

A team of scientists came, studied the disaster, shrugged, and said that a particle of antimatter had most likely struck the world, setting off a vast explosion and killing everything.

Welch wanted to know why this had occurred. The scientists told him it was pure accident. A freak of fate. Nothing more.

From that moment on, Welch ceased to believe in the idea of orderly fate. He refused to consider that any act might be predestined. His vision of the universe changed from a sight of total order to one of total chaos.

He soon realized that if he was not to be paralyzed by constant fear, he must do something himself to control the disorder that surrounded him. If God could not manipulate the universe, then he must do it himself.

He settled on Paradise Planet—the most controllable environment in the galaxy—and developed his own talents. Within a few years, nothing surprised him. When something around him happened, it was because he had made it happen.

He understood that wealth equaled power, which equaled manipulation. For that reason, he had manipulated Kail Kaypack into undertaking a galactic voyage. The soul purpose of that voyage—though no one else understood this—was to allow Rickard Welch to better control the chaos around him.

But then the beast had come. In an instant, Welch had understood: the beast could never be controlled.

And he hated the beast—he feared the beast.

But something even worse was happening now: Kaypack was showing that he, too, could no longer be controlled.

The beast was the particle of antimatter, and now Kaypack was the beast.

Satisfied that no one had seen him enter this room, Welch now reached into the dark recesses of a floor cabinet. His fingers twitched, grasping, and he soon felt the cool, comforting steel.

He removed the nervegun, checked to see that it was loaded, and thrust the weapon into a pocket.

Once he had believed in God's ability to control destiny. Then he had believed in his own.

Both God and man shared one aspect: both could kill.

Welch knew he must be ready.

Nova peered across the length of the control room to where Darcey sat studying Helsing's new charts. She looked at the back of his head, the twisted knots of hair, and at his thin shoulders.

I think I'm in love with him, she thought suddenly. She laughed aloud in sheer surprise. By God, I am.

"Darcey," she said in a voice that sounded new and alien even to her own ears, "would you mind coming over here for a moment?"

He turned and looked at her. (She'd never noticed those funny, floppy ears before.) "Sure, Nova."

He stood.

She laughed. (From fear this time.)

The Simerians sat, cuddling and cooing. The universe swirled around them and they waited unmoved. It happened. It did not happen.

In time, they knew, this sleep would end, and then the pain would flow anew.

According to the navigation charts piled before him, Johann Helsing understood that the *Arjuna* would, some eight common days from now, reach a point in grayspace where a jump could be made that would bring the ship within a mere billion miles of an inhabited world.

What confused him was that his past feelings were in no way affected by this knowledge.

Helsing remained convinced that some sort of final ending was drawing nearer with each passing moment.

Yet, when would it finally come?

Turning in his chair, he gazed at the four viewscreens within the control room. For the first time in many weeks, he actually searched for the beast. He saw it once only.

But then he blinked.

Maria Novitsky stroked her round belly and grinned. She felt full. "I think if I had to starve to death," she told Nova, who lay stretched out on another bunk, "I'd rather commit suicide by holding my breath."

"Well, you don't have to worry about that anymore," Nova said, her voice showing little interest.

"Johann says four more days."

"I know. But won't you—" Nova turned, her uncertainty showing, "in a way, won't you miss it?"

"The beast?" said Maria, but there was no reason to ask. She nodded and touched her stomach again. "Yes, I think I will."

While the Simerians hugged each other behind him, Veador continued to gaze at the fusion engine. In another two common days, the motor would be expected to function again. He didn't want anything to go wrong. His commander had directed him to take care, and for Veador, who had discovered the presence of order among chaos through the simple means of personal loyalty, nothing else could possibly matter.

Alone in his stateroom, too aware of the passage of time to need a clock, Kail Kaypack recalled vividly how the agonizing waves of fear had swept through his soul the first time he set eyes upon the beast.

Had he ever believed until then? It seemed instead that the grayspace beast had merely existed for him as a steady factor. It was part of an old dream. As a young man, he had traveled through grayspace, and as an old man, he had been denied that joy. When he spoke of the beast, he had remembered the rest of it—the parts that had once been real—and if it had finally taken the grayspace beast to evoke those old, dead memories, then he had—at least for those moments—believed firmly in the beast.

In fact, he didn't think it was until he had actually seen the beast and known it was real that he understood that he had never believed in it before.

Then came the mad chase. Why that? Darcey, he knew, was the simple reason. To have refused to chase the beast at that time would have meant committing the one act his soul could not have borne: he would have shown fear in front of Darcey.

Of course, that was why he had finally devised the scheme of going to Radius. He had thought he'd known what would happen there. The Radians would bluntly refuse to discuss the question and because of that the matter of the beast could be ended.

Then Sung had fooled him. Sung had told—not himself but Darcey.

It was then that he had realized what should have been staring him in the face all along. He wasn't merely old, he was too old. If he feared this beast, it could be for no other reason than that he feared dying, and if dying was right for him rather than wrong, then there was no longer any reason why he should be afraid.

So he wasn't afraid. He wanted to hunt the beast. And, when Nova made it possible for him to do just that, when his scheme to ensure her opposition backfired, he was glad.

When the beast appeared—and he never for an instant doubted that it would—even now, with only a single common day remaining before jump, he would venture out alone to meet it.

He expected to find one of two things when this happened: either the truth or his own death.

It was even possible he might find both.

Darcey was his son.

I eagerly anticipated the explosion certain to be generated by that particular revelation, and when I was greeted by nothing but silence, my mouth fell open several gaping inches. "But he's not joking," I finally managed. "I know it was done clumsily but I wanted to surprise you. Darcey is Kaypack's natural son, his only son. Nori knew it, probably Sten too, but not Darcey. Why do you think the Radians sent him back to Kaypack?"

"You've miscounted," said one of them. "Kaypack, Nori, Sten, and this roomful."

I couldn't act other than astonished. "You knew?"

"Since I don't know how many hours ago. Now cut the dumb, obvious revelations and get on with the story."

Cut to the quick (and damn proud, too), I did just that.

Maria Novitsky and Johann Helsing stood watch when the grayspace beast at last appeared.

The time stood a mere seven common hours before jump. Helsing, who saw the beast first, blinked and blinked. The beast wavered once, then grew steadily in size. When the glittering silver shape filled one full corner of the screen, Helsing spun and yelped, "It's here."

Maria turned quickly and, seeing the beast, laughed. "Well, I'll be damned. Look who's here."

She turned at once to call Commander Kaypack.

Darcey heard of none of this until later. The harsh tickling of fingers against his spine roused him from a deep, dream-ridden slumber.

Opening his eyes, he saw Nova. The passion upon her face held no secrets.

"The beast!" cried Darcey, sitting up. "It's here!"

Nova nodded. She jerked Darcey to his feet. "We've got

to hurry. He's already on his way to the shuttle bay and won't listen to reason. He still intends to go out alone."

"So?" said Darcey, puzzled through his excitement. "He always said he would."

"I know, but I thought—don't you think?—maybe we ought to go with him."

Darcey grinned with joy. "Do you really mean that?"

Nova shrugged. "Sure, why not? We know what the beast really is—he doesn't."

Darcey ran for his clothes and struggled to dress.

Nova stood in the doorway. "Hurry up or we'll miss him."

"Where are the others?" he asked as they raced side by side through the narrow, twisting corridor that led to the shuttle bay in the belly of the ship.

"Helsing and Maria must still be in the control room. Veador and the Simerians, as far as I know, haven't left the engine room. That leaves only Welch, and I haven't seen him since it happened. I thought he was with you."

"He was," said Darcey, "when I fell asleep. But the beast—where is it?"

She threw up her hands in an expression that might have indicated joy. "Not more than this far from the ship. It fills both the rear screens. Darcey, you wouldn't believe it, that thing is enormous."

"And evil," he said, more realistically.

"So they say."

"You don't believe Sung?"

"I don't disbelieve him."

Something puzzling in her tone told him not to press the point. Besides, unlike Kaypack, he had never really felt that anything about the beast mattered except its firm existence.

And no one doubted that anymore.

They reached the shuttle bay just in time to see Commander Kaypack inserting his left leg into the cockpit of a shuttle. Darcey recognized the particular craft as the only one of the three shuttles that was actually armed.

"Commander Kaypack!" he called. "Wait—it's us!"

Kaypack, never looking up, reached for his hip. He clutched a nervegun and pointed it at Darcey. "Get out of here," he ordered.

"But, sir." Surprised and frightened, Darcey tried to edge forward. "We want to go with you."

Nova clutched his shirt and whispered, "Stay still—he's not kidding."

Kaypack looked sad. "I'm sorry, Darcey, but I can't permit that. This is something I've got to do alone."

"But we're not afraid."

Kaypack had not lowered his weapon. "I don't think you are, but use your head. If both of us are killed, what then? Somebody has to stay alive to command the ship."

"Veador can."

"No, not Veador. It has to be you."

"But you don't know what the beast is, sir. Nova and I do. You have to let us come along."

Kaypack shook his head. For a brief moment, the nervegun seemed to waver. "I know all I need to know," Kaypack said.

Then Nova screamed.

Spinning in surprise, Darcey saw Rickard Welch charge into the room. He held a nervegun clutched in one hand and waved it threateningly in the air. Commander Kaypack must have seen all this, too, but Welch fired first. An instant later, Kaypack fired, too. Welch screamed, fell forward, and skidded across the floor like a slippery boot.

The body came to rest inches from where Nova stood. She crouched down, felt the wrist, and said, "He's dead."

But Darcey looked elsewhere. He pointed to Kaypack, who lay sprawled beside the shuttle. "I think—he can't be dead."

Nova went over to find out. She moved carefully, like a swimmer under water. When she let go of Kaypack's limp wrist, she said, "Yes."

Darcey felt the sting of his tears. Without knowing why,

he shook his fists at the high ceiling. "You bastards, how could you be so cruel? You let him come so close—and now this."

"It wasn't them," Nova said soothingly. She pointed at the body nearest Darcey. "It was Welch."

"Oh, to hell with Welch. Can't you see how wasted this is?"

"Why?" she said, coming toward him.

"Because it isn't—"

She gripped his wrist. "Don't tell me." She spoke softly. "Tell the beast."

Inside the shuttle, Darcey used the panel communicator to call Veador in the engine room and tell him that Kaypack was dead.

Veador showed no emotion—not even surprise. "How?" he asked.

"Welch killed him—with a nervegun."

"And Welch himself?" Veador asked.

"Dead, too. They must have fired almost simultaneously."

"Then I must return to Maya," Veador said.

More so than at any other moment since he'd known Veador, Darcey understood that he was not and never could be a human being. Yet, in spite of his surface coolness, Veador, Darcey believed, mourned his commander's death. "You don't intend to leave right away."

"I referred to the period subsequent to our jump."

"Nova and I are going after the beast ourselves."

"I assumed as much. You'll want me to open the bay doors."

"Yes."

"Should I notify the control room?"

"You should. And, Veador, if I die—if we die—then take the *Arjuna* to the nearest planet and sell it."

Darcey had anticipated some form of protest. Veador said, "I will use the proceeds to pay for my scan to Maya."

"Yes," said Darcey. "Yes, do that."

"Certainly, my commander."

Darcey shut down the viewscreen.

"He's got all the feelings of an old snake," Nova said.

"No," said Darcey. "His feelings aren't any different from ours. I think they just come out differently."

When the bay doors slid open, exposing the shuttle to open grayspace, Darcey immediately drew back the cockpit lever that released the shuttle from the grip of the berth. He slowly eased the hand throttle forward and then to the left. With a shrill groan, the shuttle jerked away. Darcey aimed for the open bay. The shuttle bounced off one side with a sharp crack, then slipped into grayspace.

"You haven't flown this before, have you?" said Nova.

"No, have you?"

"Nope."

"Then I might as well be the one."

"Sure." She laid a hand on his shoulder and pinched the bone. "And good luck to you, my commander."

Darcey grinned. "You think luck will help?"

"What else? I've seen people get rich on luck alone."

"We're not trying to get rich."

The beast now nestled near the stern of the ship, so Darcey boldly turned the shuttle in that direction. From out here, he studied the ancient dents pocking the *Arjuna*'s bronze hull, the ugly swollen rivets and jagged joints. He told himself it was wrong to expect a ship of this type to be beautiful. Form followed function, and that was a beauty of its own. Or ought to be. The vacuum of grayspace swarmed through the window inches ahead. An odd, mellow, restful mood took control of Darcey. He might have been listening to a gentle symphony. Nova clutched his free hand. He pressed her palm, worn and ragged from weeks of scrub work. He thought he saw her smile.

Then, through the window, he finally saw the grayspace beast, and his mood was transformed.

To have called it merely huge would have approached telling a lie. Compared to, say, a moon or planet or small star—on the cosmic scale, that is—the beast was not a large stellar object. To have described it as silver would not have been fully accurate, either. Seen from this close, the beast did not reflect any single color. Instead, it resembled a sort of transparent, wispy cloud formed from many separate particles, and each of these particles glittered a different shade—some red, others blue, many green, violet, or yellow. Seen as a whole, from any significant distance, the effect produced was a silver one. But here—this close—each separate particle pulsed like a compressed bolt of poised lightning.

"I'm frightened," Nova said.

"I am, too," said Darcey.

But he continued to drive the shuttle toward the beast. He heard Nova cry out beside him but ignored the noise. The beast hovered, unmoving, a bare distance ahead. At last, drawing the hand throttle toward him, Darcey stalled the shuttle.

"Why did you do that?" Nova asked. She seemed quite calm again. "Aren't we going closer?"

"I thought I'd check our weapons."

She giggled. "You think that'll help? Are you planning to shoot the beast?"

"I don't think I'm planning anything." Which was true: he could only proceed, move forward.

"What weapons do we carry?"

"A couple of large nerveguns. Some gas grenades. There's a firebomb and some raw explosives."

"Not even anything nuclear?"

He grinned. "The *Arjuna* is an exploratory craft, not a war vessel."

"Then how are we going to fight that thing?"

"With our brains, I suppose."

"From way out here." She gestured vaguely toward the

window. Like Darcey, she clearly preferred to look anywhere but there. The beast was simply too awesome.

"No, in there."

"You mean go inside?"

"I don't see any other way."

For the first time, Nova showed real fear. "I don't think I
can do that, Darcey—go in there. Not unless—unless you
have a good reason for doing it."

He could have told her—honestly—that there was nothing
else to try. Relying upon the secret knowledge they shared,
he said, "If the beast is alive—and we know it is—then there
must be something—a heart or brain or soul—that permits it
to live, that contains the real lifeforce. If we can find that and
wound it or kill it, then we'll have succeeded."

Nova shook her head bluntly. "Not necessarily. This beast
may be totally different from anything else in the universe.
How do we know how it lives?"

He knew she was right. "But we have to find out."

"I suppose we do."

"And we can't from out here."

"True."

"Then we have to go in."

"I suppose that's logical. The trouble is, that thing isn't."

"We have to hope it is—at least a little bit."

"I understand."

He knew he would get no greater commitment from her.
Darcey reached forward and drew the hand throttle toward
his seat. The shuttle edged forward. Darcey dropped the
lever that locked the throttle into position. He didn't want to
trust his own hand to continue the charge. He looked out the
forward window. The image of the beast stretched everywhere, glittering in rainbow-speckled shades. Beyond this vision, nothing existed for certain.

Darcey peered closer, forcing his eyes to observe. He noticed that the particles composing the beast seemed to drift in
steady orbits, but none of these paths appeared to bear any

relation to another. The effect produced, in spite of the surface order, was one of watching specks of dust blown by a massive storm. Nova held his hand again. Could she be watching, too? The particles banged against the forward window, orbits going askew. Darcey threw up his free hand and tried to shield his eyes. Nova whimpered, stiffened, and drew back.

Darcey realized the shuttle had now entered the bulk of the beast.

They were swallowed.

What was here? Inside? Darcey strained to see, but nothing showed distinctly. Visions appeared in the corners of his eyes, but when he swiveled his head to see directly, the visions vanished. It was many moments before he understood that life existed here. Creatures. Radians? Tall, gray-skinned creatures danced ambiguously back and forth upon feet that moved in a blur of swiftness. He saw trees, rivers, wide oceans. Huge silver cities climbed toward a golden sky. Airships flew. There was more—all equally impossible, absurd. His eyes could only observe.

This was a vision of old Radius, he finally decided. If the collective soul of one species resided here, then these maddening visions were only part of that. Was it the same on Gorgan Mount? More visions there? Did the elders climb only to uncover what he had discovered here in the vacuum of grayspace?

But then he saw that these visions, indistinct as they were, did not remain static. No, they moved, told stories, enacted dramas. Darcey felt ill. He saw rape, murder, war, slaughter, famine, death, death. My God, he felt like screaming, is this all there is? No, no, he cautioned himself. Sung was right. Only evil resides here. The portion driven out. He continued to watch this utter horror. "I am here in a shuttle," he said aloud. "What I see out there is not real. This shuttle is real, its control panel and instruments. Nova is real, and so am I."

Then he saw the vision of a rainbow-flaming rocket bursting through a blue sky to freedom.

Nova, beside him, moaned at the beauty.

Was this part of the evil, too?

"Turn the shuttle."

He recognized Nova's voice. "What?" He watched the rocket through its crest.

"Over there. On the sides. There's more. Turn the shuttle."

The rocket fell mournfully.

"Turn it!"

A second rocket—one more beautiful than the first, as sleek and silver as a steel pillar—rose in an arc.

Nova reached out, grabbed the steering controls, and gave them a frantic jerk to the left. The sudden change in the shuttle's direction jolted Darcey. He fell against the straps that bound him to his seat.

"Now look!" Nova cried exultantly. "There's more—I knew there was."

Darcey, seeing, threw his hands in front of his eyes and screamed.

Nova was screaming, too, but would not look away. "It's the rest of it, Darcey. The part we didn't want to see. It's us."

In a burst of self-control, Darcey lowered his hands, sealed his lips, and stared.

The creatures were dancing again, frantic feet flying.

He recognized one as himself.

All his life, while fast asleep, no different from any other man, Darcey had been chased by private demons dredged up from a slumbering unconscious. These same nightmare visions also existed here. He saw the evil that was within them, recognized it fully as his own, and felt disgust and loathing. Nova sat transfixed. Did she see what he saw, or was she visited by personal monsters all her own?

Darcey saw the evil that was Darcey, and Nova saw her own.

Was this the grayspace beast?

He saw her hands reach up to clutch her own throat, and he knew her supreme will had at last failed her. Breaking free from a spell of his own, Darcey gripped her wrists and drew them down. He screamed at her ear: "We can bear it—we can. It's not real. Don't worry."

But even as he spoke he knew that was a lie. The visions streamed before his eyes. It is real, he thought. Oh, my God, it must be.

Darcey understood at last that there was a way to kill the beast. He held his own wrists and refused to be tempted.

Nova screamed again and again.

She also knew.

"So that's it," said a student. "All that long, long story just to reach that point." He shook his head but I don't think he was sorry. "The grayspace beast is us."

"Or you," I said.

"Or me," he agreed.

"Then the Radians were mistaken," a girl said. "That whole story they told Darcey and Nova—it wasn't right."

"For them it was," I said.

"Then they didn't lie?"

"Oh, no," I said. "They lied, all right."

"But why? That wasn't fair."

"Do you think Kaypack, Nova, Maria, even Darcey—do you think they would have gone hunting for the beast if they'd known what it was?"

"It still wasn't fair."

I shrugged. "No, but there are other, better ways now."

"What do you mean by that?"

"Let's wrap up the story first," I suggested.

When Darcey awoke in his bunk aboard the *Arjuna*, he first reached frantically down and gripped the mattress beneath him in an attempt to prevent his body from tumbling free through the void of grayspace.

Then he noticed Maria Novitsky dangling in the air above

him. Somehow her puzzled smile reassured him that the danger was gone.

He let go of the mattress and did not fall.

"So you are alive," Maria said. "We'd begun to worry."

"Nova?" said Darcey. She hadn't heard. He struggled to draw enough breath to speak. "Nova!" This time his voice seemed to bellow.

But she heard him. "Nova's fine. She's up in the control room with Helsing. They're going over our charts before setting off."

"But she's all right—she's alive?"

"Now who," said Maria, "do you think brought you back here?"

A memory visited his mind, a stray wisp of the past. "The beast caught us."

"It's gone."

"We couldn't get out."

"You're here now."

"But what—how did it happen?"

"Nova could tell you better than me. We watched the shuttle on the screens. We saw you enter the beast and then much later—we were pretty worried by then—you came out. The shuttle stalled, so Veador and I went out and fetched you. Nova was in pretty bad shape and you were much worse. That was three common days ago."

"Three days!"

"Give or take a couple of hours." She pushed him down and stood herself. "Don't fret. Everything's running as smooth as a clock. I'll tell Nova you're awake."

"But the beast—" He tried to shout after her. "If it comes back, if it—"

Only her voice reached him: "It won't."

Then he was alone again.

The next time Darcey opened his eyes, it was Nova's smiling face that hung suspended in the air. She sat down beside him and said, "Good morning, my commander."

He had trouble understanding. His memories—some stayed far away. "I'm not the commander."

"Kaypack's dead—don't you remember?"

"No—yes." He spoke softly.

"That makes you commander. So how do you feel?"

"Better. I think I can remember. The grayspace beast. We went inside, didn't we?"

Her eyes burned with a fearful recollection. "Yes."

"And you brought us out?"

She showed the faintest smile. "I must have. You passed out. I took the controls. Eventually—time has no meaning inside that thing—we came out. When I looked back, the beast was gone. Later I woke up here—the same as you. It was two days, not three."

"But the beast."

"They say it went away. I don't know."

"Sung lied to us."

She nodded solemnly. "I know he did."

"The beast isn't just them. They're in there, but it's us, too —it must be everything. We tried to kill it"—he laughed bitterly—"and that was so stupid."

She stared at him. "Was it?"

"You can't kill something like that."

"How do you know? It ran away—didn't it?—we stayed and fought. Why would Sung have sent you here if the whole thing was impossible?"

"Maybe he didn't know as much as we do now."

"That may be true, but it still doesn't mean we should just give up. Look, Darcey, the beast exists. That's what we know for certain and it's what we've got to cling to. It's not a mythical creature, a figment of imagination, or anything mystical either. It exists, it lives, it can be killed. I've been thinking a lot about this. Men have been in space for centuries and in that time they've been lucky. Except for the Radians, maybe, they've met nothing they couldn't understand. That made men cocky, overconfident, weak. The beast is something way beyond our understanding, and that's why it's so damn important."

"Now you sound like Kaypack."

"Why not? As crazy as he was, he wasn't stupid. I know that now, the same as I know the beast better. So do you, Darcey. Kaypack was right all along. Remember, he said you couldn't kill it if you didn't understand it, but he was wrong because you can't understand something like the beast just by asking Sung. We have to chase it, attack it, go in again and again, die if we have to. In the end, damn it, we will win."

He could not have been more astonished if she'd declared her undying love for Veador. "But they won't let us—the crew."

She laughed happily. "Now that's our fault once again. You don't know how proud they are. Helsing, Maria, even Veador. We met the beast and did not run. Sure, they're afraid. You and I are, too—a lot more afraid. But they won't quit. Talk to them. You're their commander. They'll follow you, Darcey—I know it."

"Then—then—" He found it difficult to speak.

She grinned widely. "Yes?"

"Then we go on," he said.

Finished at last, I stood up and moved casually across to the control panel. I could tell they were brimming with questions, complaints, comments, and criticism, but the fact was I'd already explained too much already.

I ignored their plaintive shouts and cries, except for one pretty girl, whose question I could easily guess in advance. (It was the one thing throughout the whole story that had really concerned her.) "Now will you admit that you are Darcey?" she said, most predictably.

I had lived through this moment so many times before, and yet the pleasure of anticipation had barely diminished. Grinning, I laid a hand upon the lever that activated the screens and said, "My name is Sung."

While they gasped, I jerked the switch. Their eyes were slow in comprehending. Three screens showed the same gray wastes.

In the fourth, a glittering silver speck, the grayspace beast, floated, awaiting the newest generation.